Bamba Suso and Banna Kanute

The Sunjata Story

TRANSLATED BY GORDON INNES AND
BAKARI SIDIBE

PENGUIN EPICS

PENGUIN BOOKS

Published by the Penguin Group
Penguin Books Ltd, 80 Strand, London WC2R 0RL, England
Penguin Group (USA) Inc., 375 Hudson Street, New York, New York 10014, USA
Penguin Group (Canada), 90 Eglinton Avenue East, Suite 700, Toronto, Ontario, Canada M4P 2Y3
(a division of Pearson Penguin Canada Inc.)
Penguin Ireland, 25 St Stephen's Green, Dublin 2, Ireland (a division of Penguin Books Ltd)
Penguin Group (Australia), 250 Camberwell Road, Camberwell, Victoria 3124, Australia
(a division of Pearson Australia Group Pty Ltd)
Penguin Books India Pvt Ltd, 11 Community Centre, Panchsheel Park, New Delhi – 110 017, India
Penguin Group (NZ), cnr Airborne and Rosedale Roads, Albany,
Auckland 1310, New Zealand (a division of Pearson New Zealand Ltd)
Penguin Books (South Africa) (Pty) Ltd, 24 Sturdee Avenue,
Rosebank, Johannesburg 2196, South Africa

Penguin Books Ltd, Registered Offices: 80 Strand, London WC2R 0RL, England

www.penguin.com

This translation of *The Sunjata Story* first published 1974
The extracts in this edition first published in Penguin Books 1999
This extract published in Penguin Books 2006

1

Translation copyright © Gordon Innes, 1974, 1999
All rights reserved

The moral right of the translator has been asserted

Taken from the Penguin Classics edition of *The Sunjata*,
translated by Gordon Innes and Bakari Sidibe

Typeset by Rowland Phototypesetting Ltd, Bury St Edmunds, Suffolk
Printed in England by Clays Ltd, St Ives plc

ISBN-13: 978-0-141-02685-5
ISBN-10: 0-141-02685-5

Contents

Note

Sunjata Keita was the founder of one of the greatest empires of Western Africa. These two accounts of his life tell how Sunjata defeated his Susu overlords and created the Mali Empire which would last for two centuries. Based on events from the early thirteenth century, these tales of magic and heroism are still celebrated across West Africa as part of a living epic oral tradition. These two versions of Sunjata's story are translations of live performances by two leading Gambian *jalis* (or bards). The first version, by Bamba Suso, centres on the human relationships of the story while the second, by Banna Kanute, emphasizes the violent action and supernatural forces.

Bamba Suso: Sunjata

It is I, Bamba Suso, who am talking,
Along with Amadu Jebate;
It is Amadu Jebate who is playing the *kora*,
And it is I, Bamba Suso, who am doing the talking.
Our home is at Sotuma;
That is where we both were born;
This tune that I am now playing,
I learned it from my father,
And he learned it from my grandfather.
Our grandfather's name – Koriyang Musa.
That Koriyang Musa
Went to Sanimentereng and spent a week there;
He met the jinns, and brought back a *kora*.
The very first *kora*
Was like a *simbingo*.
The *kora* came from the jinns.
Amadu Jebate's father's name was Griot Fili Jebate.
He came from Gaali in the East,
But the name of the area was Gaadugu.
My father, Griot Musa,
And Griot Fili were the sons of two sisters.
When my own father died it was Griot Fili who took
     my mother;
It was he whom I knew as my father.
All right,

I am going to tell you the story of Sunjata,
And you must pay attention.
Sunjata's father's name was Fata Kung Makhang.
He went to Sankarang Madiba Konte.
The soothsayers had said, 'If you go to Sankarang
    Madiba Konte
And find a wife there,
She will give birth to a child
Who will become king of the black people.'
He went there.
They had told him the name of this woman;
They called her Sukulung.
Nine Sukulungs were brought forward,
And a soothsayer consulted the omens,
And then declared, 'No, I do not see the woman
    among these ones.'
They said to Sankarang Madiba Konte,
'Now, is there not another Sukulung?'
He answered, 'There is, but she is ugly.
She is my daughter.'
He told him, 'Go and bring her here; I wish to see
    her.'
When they had brought her,
A soothsayer consulted the omens and then told him,
    'This is the one.'
When Fata Kung Makhang had married her in
    Manding,
Then he and she went away.
She became pregnant, and for seven years
Sunjata's mother was pregnant with him.
She did not get a fright even once,

Except for one occasion.
Her husband called her,
During the rainy season, and he happened to speak at
    the same time that thunder sounded,
So that she did not hear him speak, and he repeated
    the call.
Then she went in trepidation to her husband.
That was the only fright that she ever got;
For seven years she never got a fright,
Except for that one occasion.
She gave birth to Sunjata.
The king had declared,
Fata Kung Makhang had declared, 'If any of my wives
    gives birth to a son,
I shall give my kingship to him.'
Sukulung Konte eventually gave birth –
Sunjata's mother.
They sent a slave, with the instructions, 'Go and tell
    Sunjata's father.'
At that time he had built a compound out on the farm
    land.
When the slave came he found them eating,
And they said to him, 'All right, sit down and have
    something to eat.'
The slave sat down.
It was not long before a co-wife of Sukulung's also
    gave birth.
When her co-wife gave birth, they sent a griot.
When the griot arrived he said, 'Greetings!'
They said to him, 'Come and have something to eat
    before you say anything.'

He said, 'No!'
The griot said, 'Naareng Daniyang Konnate,
Your wife has given birth – a boy.'
The slave was sitting; he said, 'They sent me first.
It was Sukulung Konte who gave birth first.'
Fata Kung Makhang declared,
'The one I heard of first,
He it is who is my son, the firstborn.'
That made Sunjata angry.
For seven years he crawled on all fours,
And refused to get up.
Those seven years had passed,
And the time had come for the boys who were to be
    circumcised to go into the circumcision hut.
People said, 'But Sunjata is crawling on all fours and
    has not got up;
The time to go into the circumcision hut has arrived,
    and all his brothers are going in.'
At that time they used to smelt ore and make iron
    from it;
The smiths put bellows to the ore,
And when they had smelted the ore they made it into
    iron,
And they forged the iron and made it into rods –
Two rods.
They put one into one of his hands,
And they put the other into his other hand,
And said that he must get up.
When he had grasped the rods, they both broke.
They said, 'How will Sunjata get up?'
He himself said to them, 'Call my mother;

4

When a child has fallen down, it is his mother who
    picks him up.'
When his mother came,
He laid his hand upon his mother's shoulder,
And he arose and stood up.
It is from that incident that the griots say,
'The Lion has arisen,' they say, 'The Lion of Manding
    has arisen,
The mighty one has arisen.'
There were trousers in Manding;
Whoever was to be king of Manding,
If they put those trousers on you,
And you were able to get up with them on,
Then you would become king of Manding.
But if they put those trousers on you,
And you did not get up with them on,
Then you would not be king of Manding.
They brought those trousers,
But whichever of his brothers they put them on,
He was unable to get up with them on.
When they brought them to Sunjata,
They were trying to put them on Sunjata,
But the trousers did not fit Sunjata – they were too
    small –
Until a bit was added.
After that had happened they went into the
    circumcision shed.
After they had come out of there,
It was not long before his father died.
Sunjata announced, 'As for myself,
However extensive my father's property may be,

I want no part of it except the griots.'
They asked him, 'Do you want the griots?'
They said, 'Leave it;
A person who has nothing will not have griots for
    long.'
The griots said, 'Since he has let all his inheritance go,
And says that it is only us that he wants,
We will not abandon him.
If he does not die, we shall not desert him.'
The griots were at his side.
It happened that three things were distinctive in
    Sunjata's family:
They had three hairs on their body, and if you spoke
    the names of those hairs,
Whoever was a legitimate child would die that year.
The griots said, 'Ah, he has absolutely nothing,
So let us employ some guile and if he dies, then we can
    take it easy,
And go to men of substance.'
They went and begged from him.
When they went and begged from him,
He did not have anything.
He went and got honey in the bush,
And brought it back for the griots.
Whatever he gave them, they did not scorn it.
They went off; that is why the griots call him
*Bee, little bee, Makhara Makhang Konnate, Haimaru and
    Yammaru.*
Next morning they came and begged from him.
He had nothing,
So he went and caught a cat and gave it to them;

That is why the griots call him
Cats on the shoulder Simbong.
The griots came and begged from him again.
And he had nothing,
So he went and found some firewood in the bush and
    came back and gave it to them.
From that incident the griots say,
'*Firewood Makhara Makhang Konnate, Haimaru and
    Yammaru,*
The lion is full of dignity, the resilient hunter.'
The griots came and begged from him again.
He went and took a strip of cloth.
What he took was to the value of one shilling and
    sixpence.
It belonged to his brothers,
But no one dared to apprehend him
Because no one dared to stand up to him.
He gave it to the griots,
Who said, 'Jata has committed a theft';
It was that which gave him the name Sunjata;
His name was Makhang Konnate.
His name became Sunjata
When he took the one-and-sixpenny strip of cloth
And gave it to the griots.
They knew that he had taken it,
But no one dared to ask him about it.
The griots said, 'Jata has committed theft';
It was that which gave him the name Sunjata;
His name was Makhang Konnate,
Naareng Makhang Konnate –
That was his name.

*

Then that is how things were;
His brothers got together,
And then they went to a sorcerer
And told him, 'Attack him with *korte* till he dies.'
They gave a bull to the sorcerers.
They took this bull on to a hillside;
The sorcerers congregated,
Their leader was sitting;
One was saying, 'If I attack him in the morning, by
    evening he will be dead.'
Another was saying, 'If I attack him,
When he sees the roofs of the town, he will die.'
From that the Easterners say even today,
    'Home-person-taking.'
He himself was a hunter at that time.
He left the hunting area, having killed two elephants,
Whose tails he had in his hand.
He encountered the sorcerers on the hillside.
And he greeted them, but they did not answer him.
To the leader of the sorcerers he said,
'You ought to return my greeting.
When one freeborn person greets another,
He should return the greeting.
I have killed two elephants,
One of which is lying on the hillside.'
He took its tail out of his bag and threw it to them,
He said, 'I give it to you,
For you to add to your own meat.
But what you were sent to do,
Just do it!'
As he was about to go,

The leader of the sorcerers called him.
When he came, he said to him,
'You must leave Manding.
If someone says he will kill you,
A man's life is not in another man's hands,
But if he says he will ruin you,
Even if he does not ruin you, he could greatly hinder
    the fulfilment of your destiny,
It could be greatly delayed.'
Sunjata said, 'I cannot go,
My mother is at home.'
That was Sukulung Kutuma.
Hence the griots say, '*Sukulung Kutuma's child Sukulung
    Yammaru,*
Cats on the shoulder Simbong and Jata are at Naarena.'
Sunjata said, 'I cannot go;
My sister is at home.'
That was Nyakhaleng Jumo Suukho.
He said, 'My horn is at home,
My wine gourd is at home,
My bow is at home.'
The sorcerer said to him, 'I will summon all of them to
    the *korte* horn,
And they will answer the call.'
He called all of them to the *korte* horn and they
    answered the call.
He told Sunjata, 'Go!'
Sunjata's leaving Manding
And going to foreign lands came about in this manner.
On his way he came to a fork in the road,
He put down the *korte* horn and consulted it.

It told him, 'This road goes to Sankarang Madiba
    Konte,
This other road leads to Tamaga Jonding Keya' –
He was the ancestor of the Darbos.
Sunjata said, 'I shall go to Tamaga Jonding Keya's
    place,
Because if I go to the residence of my grandfather's
    sons,
My cousins and I are bound to end up quarrelling.'
He set off.
He reached Tamaga Jonding Keya's place,
And he found that they had put beeswax in a pot,
And the pot was boiling.
They took a ring and threw it into the hot wax,
And they were making their boasts on it.
This is what they were saying.
'If I am to become king of Manding,
When I plunge my hand into this boiling wax,
Let it not burn me.
But if I am not to be king of Manding,
When I plunge my hand into it,
Let my hand be destroyed.'
He found them making this declaration.
That was a public challenge.
Sunjata came and when he reached them,
He plunged his hand into that hot wax,
And took out the ring,
Threw it into cold water,
And gave it to Tamaga Jonding Keya.
Tamaga Jonding Keya was angry.
He said to Sunjata, 'There is a silk-cotton tree here;

If you are freeborn,
If you are legitimate –
We must go and shoot that silk-cotton tree.
Whoever misses that silk-cotton tree,
Whose arrow does not touch it,
Is not freeborn,
Is not legitimate.'
Sunjata was outraged
At the very thought that anyone should say to him in
    Manding,
'You are not legitimate.'
He went and drew his bow and shot the silk-cotton
    tree.
Tamaga Jonding Keya also drew his bow
And shot the silk-cotton tree.
Sunjata went and pulled out his arrow,
And said, 'If my mother was pregnant with me for
    seven years,
And she never had a fright,
Then when I shoot this silk-cotton tree, let it fall
    down.'
He shot the silk-cotton tree –
The tree remained standing.
He drew his knife,
He went and grabbed his mother's arm,
And said to her, 'Tell me about myself;
Tell me about the circumstances of my birth in
    Manding,
Otherwise I will kill you.'
Master of the lion! Master of the maga! Master of the
    rhinoceros!

Ah, cats on the shoulder,
Simbong and Jata are at Naarena.
Maabirama Konnate is no more.
Before Daniyang Konnate returned to the next world –
Naareng Daniyang Konnate has perished –
His griots were saying, 'Daniyang Konnate,
Are you afraid of death?'
He said, 'Death is not the thing I fear;
My griots must cross four great rivers,
They must cross four great swamps,
They will come to a worthless man and an even more
    worthless one,
And he will say, "Go away,
I swear I have nothing,
You are a griot,
You must get it from someone else.
Go away."'
He said, 'The dog was standing – may God lay him low,
When he is laid low, may God make him never rise again.'
Cats on the shoulder,
Simbong and Jata are at Naarena.
The world does not belong to any man.
Sunjata said to his mother,
'If I am a bastard,
Make it clear to me,
And I will kill you and kill myself.
If I am not a bastard in Manding,
Make it clear to me,
Because I shot the silk-cotton tree and it did not fall
    down,
And I had made my boast.'

She said to him, 'You went too far in your boast;
For seven years I was pregnant with you,
And I never had a fright,
But during the rainy season it was thundering,
And when your father called me I did not hear him,
And he called a second time.
That day I went in trepidation to your father.
Go and take that out of your boast and then see what
    happens.'
When he had removed that declaration from his boast,
He shot the silk-cotton tree,
And the tree leant over and was about to fall.
Tamaga Jonding Keya was standing nearby,
He shouted at the silk-cotton tree,
And the tree was about to rise up straight again,
Then Sunjata bellowed at the tree,
And it split down the middle and fell to the ground.
Even to this day when a silk-cotton tree is drying up,
It begins at the top,
It never dries up at the foot,
It begins at the top.
Tamaga Jonding Keya was angry,
And he boxed Sunjata's ear.
When he boxed Sunjata's ear,
Sunjata grabbed his arm and was about to cut his
    throat,
But Sunjata's sister came running up and stood beside
    him,
And said to him, 'When you were leaving Manding,
The soothsayers told you that you would have three
    causes for anger,

But that if you assuaged your anger by retaliating you
    would never be king of Manding.
This is one of those occasions for anger – leave it.'
That is why the wrists of the members of the Darbo
    family are not thick.
Tamaga Jonding Keya said to Sunjata, 'You are not
    going to remain here in my town,
Because anyone who is a greater man than I am
Will not remain here.'
Sunjata passed through that area
And went to Faring Burema Tunkara at Neema.
He stayed there; he was engaged in hunting,
He was engaged in hunting.
Of Sunjata's brothers who were installed as king [in
    Manding],
Any whom Susu Sumanguru did not kill by witchcraft,
He would kill in war.
If they made anyone king on Monday,
By the following Monday he would be dead,
Till all his brothers were finished,
And there remained only children.
Sunjata had a younger brother,
And they called him and told him, 'Go after your older
    brother;
His brothers are all finished,
The kingship has come to him.'
Sunjata's younger brother set off,
He kept on till he reached Neema.
When he reached Neema,
He was approaching it in the heat of the day.
He was quite exhausted when his sister caught sight of him.

One loves one's brother,
Especially after a long absence.
She ran to him
And had just taken hold of her brother,
When they both fell down.
He pushed her,
And his sister fell down.
Sunjata arrived,
Having just come from the bush,
And he saw his sister sitting with an unhappy look on
     her face,
And he asked her, 'What is the matter?'
She said, 'My brother pushed me and I fell down.'
Sunjata looked at his younger brother and he said to
     him, 'Fofana,
You will never be king of Manding.'
That was how the surname Fofana originated.
It happened that his mother was ill.
When Fofana had explained the reason for his journey,
     he said to Sunjata, 'Our brothers are all finished.
Susu Sumanguru has finished our brothers;
I was told to go for you,
So that you would come back;
The kingship of Manding has come to you.'
Sunjata stood by his mother's head
And said to her, 'Before dawn breaks tomorrow, if you
     die,
I am to be king of Manding.
As long as you remain ill,
I am not to be king of Manding,
Because I will not leave you here in illness.'

Before dawn broke, Sukulung Konte died.

Sunjata said that he would bury Sukulung Konte.

Faring Burema Tunkara told him,

'You will not bury her until you have bought the burial
    plot.'

Sunjata asked him, 'How am I to buy it?'

He said, 'You must fit earrings together,

And lay one upon her forehead,

And lay one upon her big toe,

And then measure the length on the ground;

However long the chain is, that is what you must dig,

And you will bury your mother there.'

When he had done that, he put the gold earrings
    together,

And he laid one upon his mother's forehead,

And he laid another upon her big toe,

And he measured it on the ground.

The gravediggers were about to go,

But he said to them, 'Wait!'

He took the gold and laid it on a new winnowing tray,

And he laid a broken pot on it,

He laid a bush fowl's egg on it,

He laid some old thatching grass on it,

And then he gave it to Faring Burema Tunkara.

When it had been given to Faring Burema Tunkara,

One of the latter's men was there who was called
    Makhang Know All,

And he declared, 'I know what this means.'

Makhang Say All was there;

Makhang Say All declared, 'But I will say it.'

Faring Burema Tunkara ordered him, 'Say it!'

He said, 'What Sunjata has said here
Is that a day will come
When he will smash this town of yours just like this
    broken pot;
A day will come
When old thatch will not be seen in this town of yours
Because he will burn it all;
A day will come
When bush fowls will lay their eggs on the site of your
    deserted town.
He says here is your gold.'
When he had done that, Sunjata buried his mother;
Then he and Nyakhaleng Juma Suukho,
And his younger brother,
And Bala Faaseega Kuyate
Rose up and went.
When he and Bala Faaseega Kuyate were on their way,
They had gone far into the bush,
And they had been travelling for a long time when Bala
    said, 'I am terribly hungry.'
Sunjata said, 'Wait here.'
He went into a clump of thick bush,
He examined the calf of his leg where there was plenty
    of flesh and he cut some off.
When he had cut it into thin strips, he cooked it,
Then he pounded the leaves of a medicinal shrub and
    then tied up his leg,
He applied *kuna fito* to the wound and tied it up.
He came back,
And he said to Bala, 'Here is some meat.'
He chewed the meat,

Had a drink,
And then said, 'Let's go.'
They went on for a long time;
When the wound turned septic, Sunjata was limping.
When Sunjata was limping,
Bala Faaseega Kuyate said to him,
'Naareng, why are you limping?'
Sunjata replied, 'Just let's go on.'
Bala said, 'I will not move from here until you tell me
      what the matter is.
Since the day I first met you,
I have never seen you
In the grip of such pain
That people were aware of it from your appearance;
But now you are limping.'
Sunjata said to him, 'You said you were hungry.'
He thrust his leg out of his gown,
And he told him, 'This is what I cut off and gave to
      you.'
There is a special relationship
Between the members of the Keita family and the
      members of the Kuyate family.
Even today, if a member of the Kuyate family deceives
      a member of the Keita family,
Things will go badly for him.
If a member of the Keita family deceives a member of
      the Kuyate family,
Things will go badly for him.

They carried on till they came to Dakhajala.
They stayed at Dakhajala.

Sunjata said to Bala Faaseega Kuyate,
'Haven't you called the horses for me?'
Bala asked, 'What sort of a thing is a horse?'
Sunjata said to him, 'A griot is an impatient fellow;
Just call the horses.'
Come horses! oh horses! mighty Sira Makhang,
A person who could argue with him.
Oh horses! mighty Sira Makhang,
Being dragged does not humiliate a great beast.
A long, long way through the bush, an outstanding stallion
     and a saddle,
Go quickly and come back quickly,
Giver of news from far away.
A horse is something that goes far away,
A horseman is someone who goes far away,
A horse is something that goes far away,
A horse's rein is something that goes far away,
A horse is something that goes far away,
A horseman is someone who goes far away.
A man who buys a horse never regrets it.
Ah, mighty war king,
A man who likes making deserted villages.
Many great matters have passed from the world.
Ah, you have an army.
You seize, you slay.
Maabirama Konnate, fighting goes well with you.
When he called the horses,
A white stallion appeared,
And Sunjata said, 'This is a fine-looking horse,
But if it falls ill, it will not recover.'
The griot called the horses,

And a brownish horse with white lower legs appeared,
And Sunjata said, 'I did not say this one.'
The griot called the horses,
A brownish horse with a white circle on its forehead
    appeared,
And Sunjata leapt on it first.
That is why the griots say,
'Oh horses, brownish horse.'
Sunjata told his griot, 'You must summon my leading
    men.'
Those who were known as leading men
Are what we Mandinka call army commanders,
And what the Easterners call men of death.
When he had summoned the leading men,
Kurang Karang Kama Fofana came –
A far-seeing man and a man who speaks with authority,
Kama crossed to the other side of the river with iron shoes,
Kama crossed the river with iron shoes.
He and one thousand,
Four hundred
And forty-four bowmen.
Sunjata declared, 'The time for battle has not yet
    arrived, Tira Makhang has not come.'
He told his griot, 'Call my leading men.'
Suru Bande Makhang Kamara came –
Foobali Dumbe Kamara,
Makhang Koto Kamara, Manding Saara Jong,
Jukuna Makhang Kamara, Baliya Kamara,
Makhang Nyaame Kamara, Nyaani Saara Jong.
He too came with one thousand,
Four hundred and forty-four bowmen.

Sunjata told him, 'The time for battle has not yet
    arrived, Tira Makhang has not come.'
Sunjata said to his griot, 'Call the important men.'
He called them.
Sankarang Madiba Konte came –
Sankarang Madiba Konte, Wuruwarang Kaaba and
    Dongeera,
Ganda who instils courage,
Ganda who deprives of courage,
Ganda, master of many arts.
Faa Ganda killed his in-law on Monday,
Next Monday Faa Ganda came into power;
They say that you should not give your daughter to Faa
    Ganda,
Killer of his in-law.
He and one thousand,
Four hundred,
And forty-
Four bowmen
Answered the call of Naareng Daniyang Konnate at
    Dakhajala.
Sunjata said to him, 'The time for fighting has not yet
    come, Tira Makhang has not come.'
Sankarang Madiba Konte demanded, 'Is Tira Makhang
    better than all the rest of us?'
Sunjata replied, 'He is not better than all the rest of
    you,
But he fights a morning battle,
He fights an evening battle,
And we join with him in the big battle.'
Sankarang Madiba Konte was Sunjata's grandfather;

He was angry, and he took out an arrow and fired it.
The arrow hit Muru,
It hit Murumuru,
It hit Gembe,
It hit Gembe's bold son,
It hit Seega, the Fula, in his navel.
That is why the griots say to members of the Konte
     family,
'Arrow on the navel Faa Ganda.'
They say if you see an arrow on a forehead,
It is Faa Ganda's arrow,
Because anyone who is shot in the forehead –
If anything has cut his head open –
Will not live.
Any serious illness which attacks you in the abdomen
     also never leaves you alive.
That is why they say, *'Arrow in the navel Faa Ganda,*
Arrow in the forehead Faa Ganda.'
They call him *Firer of the red arrow.*
He it was who shot the arrow
And slew Susu Sumanguru's father upon the hill.
All seven heads,
It was his arrow which smashed them all.
Sukulung Kutuma's child Sukulung Yammaru,
You are right, many great matters have passed,
Let us enjoy our time upon the earth.
A time for action, a time for speaking, a time for dying;
     knowing the world is not easy.
If you call a great man, no great man answers your call;
You must lay your hand upon the earth;
Many a great man is under the ground, a youthful king.

*Had the ground a mouth, it would say, 'Many great men are
    under me.'*
*Maabirama Konnate, cats on the shoulder, Simbong and
    Jata are at Naarena,*
Your griots suffered when you were not there.
Ah, you have an army,
You seize and you slay,
Sheikh 'Umar, man of war, war goes well for you.
(AMADU asks: At that time was Sunjata preparing to
    wage war against Susu Sumanguru?
BAMBA replies: He declared that he would not become
    king of Manding
Until he and Susu Sumanguru had first joined battle.)
They were at that point
When Soora Musa came –
Kiliya Musa,
Nooya Musa,
Wanjagha Musa,
Bera Senuma,
Sangang Senuma,
Maadikani Senuma,
Konsikaya Koli Kumba, eye red as Bureng gold.
He too with one thousand, four hundred
And forty-four bowmen
Answered the call of Sunjata Konnate at Dakhajala.
Sunjata declared, 'The time for fighting has not yet
    come, Tira Makhang has not arrived.'
Soora Musa asked him, 'Naareng, is Tira Makhang
    better than all the rest of us?'
Sunjata answered him, 'He is not better than all you
    others.

He fights a morning battle, he fights an evening battle,
Then we join with him in the big battle.'
(AMADU: Make clear to us which families, with which
    surnames,
Trace their descent from Tira Makhang.
BAMBA: When you hear the name Soora Musa,
If someone is called by the surname Dumbuya, that is
    Suuso.
If someone is called by the surname Kuruma, that is
    Suuso.
If someone is called by the surname Danjo, that is
    Suuso.
If someone is called by the surname Geyi, that is Suuso.
All of those are descended from Soora Musa.
If someone is called by the surname Njai, that is Konte.
If someone is called by the surname Jara, that is Konte.
When Tira Makhang rose up –
That Tira Makhang is the great Taraware.
....

The Tarawares' surname is Tira Makhang.
The surname Dambele is Tira Makhang.
The surname Jebate is Tira Makhang.
The surname Job is Tira Makhang.
The surname Juf is Tira Makhang.
The surname Saane is Tira Makhang.
The surname Maane is Tira Makhang.
The descendants of Tira Makhang are all scattered,
Their surnames are all changed in this way,
But the original surname of all of them was Taraware.)
Tira Makhang was descended from Smoke,
Smoke fathered Flame,

Flame fathered Charcoal,
Charcoal fathered Charcoal and Charcoal Chippings,
And the latter fathered Tarakoto Bullai Tarawara.
From that the griots say,
'Kirikisa the man who accompanies the king,
The man who rides horses to death and kills anyone who
     gainsays him.'
(AMADU: Then the warriors arrived.)
BAMBA: When Tira Makhang was coming,
He said, 'Wrap me in a shroud,
Because when I see Susu Sumanguru, either I put him
     in a shroud or he puts me in a shroud.
That is my declaration.'
He called his wives,
And he put them in mourning,
And he declared, 'When I see Susu Sumanguru,
If he does not do this to my wives, then this is what
     I will do to his wives.'
He then lay down upon a bier,
And they carried it on their heads and came and laid it
     at Sunjata's feet,
And Tira Makhang said to him, 'There is no need to
     make a speech;
As you see me,
When I see Susu Sumanguru,
Either he will kill me and they will wrap me in a
     shroud and lay me upon a bier,
Or else I will kill him and they will wrap him in a
     shroud and lay him upon a bier.'
(AMADU: At that time they were preparing for battle,
     but they had not yet set out.

BAMBA: War had not yet broken out.
At that time they were preparing for battle.)

When the leading men had responded,
The army rose up
And battle was joined at Taumbaara.
That day the fighting went well for the smith, Susu
 Sumanguru.
They met next at Umbaara,
And the fighting went well for Susu Sumanguru.
Then they met at Kankinyang.
Susu Sumanguru took a bow
And shot at Sunjata.
When the arrows fell upon Sunjata's gown,
He did this with his gown.
The griots said to him, 'Are you afraid?'
That is why the griots call him
Kubang Kubang Makhara Makhang Konnate Haimaru and
 Yammaru.
Sumanguru once shot at him with an arrow,
He dodged the arrow, and the griots said to him,
'Are you afraid of death, Naarena?'
It is from that incident that they call him *Dendending*
 Makhara Makhang Konnate,
Haimaru and Yammaru,
The lion is full of dignity, resilient hunter.
There was one occasion
When Sunjata walked very quickly,
And people thought that he was running away.
The griots said to him, 'Naareng, are you running
 away?'

The griots said to him, *'Kubang Kubang Makhara*
    Makhang Konnate,
Haimara and Yammaru,
The lion is full of dignity, resilient hunter;
If a lion had not broken his bones, a fool's wife would not be
    in need of strength.'
Fighting went on till the sun had set,
When it was evening, Sunjata's sister came to him –
    Nyakhaleng Juma Suukho –
And said, 'To be sure, hot water kills a man,
But cold water too kills a man.
Leave the smith and me together.'
She was the best-looking woman in both Susu and
    Manding.
When she had got herself ready,
She left the land of Manding and went to the land of
    Susu.
When the woman had gone some distance she reached
    Susu,
She reached Susu Sumanguru.
The gates of his fortified town –
The griots call smiths
Big kuku Tree,
Big Silk-cotton Tree,
Push-in-front Expert,
And Lift the Hammer.
Those were the names of the gateways of the fort,
They were gateways with porches.
Whenever the woman reached a gateway,
When she knocked, the guards would ask her,
'Where are you going?';

Inevitably they were all smitten with love for her,
But she would tell them, 'I am not your guest;
I am the guest of Susu Sumanguru.'
She would go and knock at another door,
Till she had passed through all the doorways.
They took her to Susu Sumanguru.
When Susu Sumanguru saw her,
He greatly desired the woman.
He welcomed her to the house,
And gave her every kind of hospitality.
Night fell,
And he and the woman were in his house.
Now, a princess of Manding
And a smith would not sleep together.
They were chatting,
Till the smith's mind turned in a certain direction,
And then she said to him, 'I am a guest;
I have come to you –
Don't be impatient.'
She said to him, 'There is something that greatly
    puzzles me;
Any army which comes to this town of yours is
    destroyed.'
Susu Sumanguru said to her,
'Ah, my father was a jinn.'
When he said that, his mother heard it,
Because Susu Sumanguru's
Mother was a human being,
But his father was a jinn.
Two women had conceived him;

As you may know, the griots praise smiths in terms of
    this,
Saying, *'Between Susuo and Dabi, take suck from two
    mothers.'*
Two women had conceived him;
When he was inside one of them,
She was fit, and people saw her going about
For a week or ten days, and the other one was ill;
When he returned to the other one,
The one he came out of became ill.
He would return inside her
For a week or ten days and people saw her around too.
That is why they called him *Between Susuo and Dabi,
    take suck from two mothers.*
But when these events were taking place,
Dabi was still alive.
When Sumanguru said to Sunjata's sister, 'My father is
    a jinn,'
The old lady appeared,
And said to him, 'Don't give away all your secrets to a
    one-night woman.'
When Susu Sumanguru's mother said that, the woman
    got up and said to him,
'I'm going, because your mother is driving me away.'
He said, 'Wait!'
He went and gave his mother some palm wine,
And she drank it, became drunk and fell asleep.
He said to Sunjata's sister, 'Let us continue with our
    chat.
She is an old lady.'

They were chatting,

And she said to him, 'Did you say that your father is a
     jinn?'

He said, 'My father is a jinn, and he lives on this hill.

This jinn has seven heads.

So long as he is alive, war will never damage this
     country.'

She said to him, 'Your father,

How can he be killed?'

He said, 'You must go and find a white chicken,

Then they must remove the spur of the white chicken,

They must pick the leaves of self-seeded guinea-corn,

They must put *korte* powder in it.

If they put that on the tip of an arrow,

And shoot it at this hill,

They will kill my father.

That is the only thing that will kill him.'

She asked him, 'Supposing they kill him?'

He replied, 'If war came, this country would be
     destroyed.'

She asked, 'Supposing this land were destroyed, what
     would happen to you?'

He said, 'I would become a whirlwind.'

She said, 'Supposing people went into the whirlwind
     with swords?'

He said, 'I would become an African fan-palm.'

She said to him, 'What if people were about to fell the
     palm?'

He said, 'I would become an ant-hill.'

She asked, 'Supposing people were about to scatter the
     ant-hill?'

He said, 'I would become a Senegalese cou –'
His heart palpitated,
And he fell silent.
The woman said to him, 'Wait,
I am going to the wash-place,
Because a woman and a man do not go to bed together
    dirty.'
(AMADU: That 'Senegalese cou –' – what was it he cut
    short there?
(BAMBA: He had cut short the name 'Senegalese
    coucal'.
Even today, if you fire at a Senegalese coucal in the
    bush,
Quite often the gun will shatter in your hands.)
Nyakhaleng Juma was in the wash-place,
And Susu Sumanguru was in bed inside the house.
After some time, he would say to her,
'Aren't you coming back today?'
At that time in Manding
They had a *korte* ring,
And when they laid it down,
And the person for whom it had been laid down spoke,
It would answer him.
It did not answer everybody,
But it would answer the person for whom it had been
    laid down.
She took off that *korte* ring
And threw it into the pot of ablution water.
When Sumanguru said, 'Aren't you coming?'
It would say to him, 'Wait;
Such is this fort of yours

That a guest who comes to you
Is completely in your hands.
You are king;
Why are you so impatient?'
When she had thrown the ring in there,
She climbed over the wall of the fort and off she went.
When she had gone, Sumanguru lay for a long time,
He had a short nap,
Then he awoke with a start
And went and looked inside the wash-place.
He said, 'I think there is more to this than just a visit to
    the wash-place.'
He did not find anyone there.
At length he came upon the *korte* ring,
But he did not see anyone.
He wept.
She reached Sunjata,
And she told him all that Sumanguru had said.
They went and found a white cock,
They found self-seeded guinea-corn,
They found *korte* powder.
That is why the members of the Kante family do not
    eat white chicken.
When they had prepared this arrow,
They gave it to Sankarang Madiba Konte.
It was Sankarang Madiba Konte who fired the arrow.
That is why the griots say, '*The head and neck of an
    arrow both with red* mananda,
Arrow on the forehead Faa Ganda.'
It was he who slew the jinn on the hill [Susu
    Sumanguru's father].

When he had slain the jinn on the hill in Susu,
The griots called him *The red arrow firer of Manding*.
Next morning the army rose up and flung itself against
    the fortified town;
It was not yet two o'clock when they smashed it.
Nyakhaleng Juma Suukho was with the army,
Since the soldiers were searching for Sumanguru.
When the head of a snake is cut off,
What remains is just a piece of rope.
They were searching for the king;
They were engaged on that, when she saw a great
    whirlwind arise,
And she shouted to them, 'That's him, don't let him
    get away!'
They rushed upon that whirlwind,
Armed men were entering it, when they saw a
    fan-palm standing.
She said to them, 'This is him!'
They rushed, and were about to fell the palm tree,
When he changed into an ant-hill.
She shouted to them, 'This is him!'
They took axes and were just about to smash the
    ant-hill to pieces,
When they saw a Senegalese coucal fly up
And go into an area of thick bush.
Manda Kante,
Saamagha Kante,
Tunkang Kante,
Baayang Kante,
Sege and Sirimang,
It is forging and the left hand,

33

Between Susuo and Dabi,
Frustrater of plots.
It went into thick bush.
This was how Susu Sumanguru's career ended.
That is where my own knowledge ends.
Then Sunjata took control of Susu and Manding.
The mode of life of people at that time
And our mode of life at the present day are not the
    same.
Surnames did not exist.
All the surnames with which we are familiar
Were given by Sunjata,
Because he was an extraordinary person.
If you had done anything noteworthy,
Then, when you appeared before him,
He would greet you with a name related to that.
At that time these Danso surnames –
There is an animal in the East,
Which is there even today, and which they call *dango*.
That *dango* denied people passage along the road;
People did not pass that way.
It was a rhinoceros: what we Westerners call a
    rhinoceros,
And which the Easterners call *dango*.
The ancestor of the Damfas killed that creature;
When he came to Sunjata, the latter called him
    Damfagha.
That was the origin of the surname Damfa.
The ancestor of the Dansos – a snake was lying across
    the road,
No one passed by that way.

The road from east to west was cut,
And it was that snake which had cut it.
The ancestor of the Dansos killed that snake;
When he came, Sunjata said to him, *'Kenyeramatigi,
road-clearing lion.'*
He added, 'It was you who opened up the road.'
He said to him, *'Road-clearing lion.'*
Even today the Mandinka say, 'So-and-so has cleared
the road in front of us.'
That was he,
That was the ancestor of the Dansos.
When Sunjata had taken over the kingship,
He told Tamaga Jonding Keya, 'Darbo,
You must give up your interest in the kingship of
Manding now.'
As you know, they call the members of the Suso family
Red Bureng Gold.
Soora Musa [Faa Koli] had been king of Manding,
And when Sunjata became king,
The old king and the new king did not trust one
another.
Soora Musa gave Sunjata a great quantity of gold.
At Tabaski, Sunjata said to him, *'Eye red as Bureng gold.'*
That was Soora Musa.
When they had killed Susu Sumanguru,
Sunjata became master of both countries.
He did not have any enemies,
He did not have any rivals.
Susu and Manding both belonged to Sunjata,
And his reign endured for a long time.

Banna Kanute: Sunjata

In this account which I give,
And which opens here,
The subject which I am going to talk about
Is the career of Makhang Sunjata,
As I have heard it,
Because the Sunjata story
Is very strange and wonderful.
You see one griot,
And he gives you an account of it one way,
And you will find that that is the way he heard it;
You see another griot,
And he gives you an account of it in another way,
And you will find that what he has heard has
    determined his version.
What I have myself heard,
What I have heard from my parents,
That is the account which I shall put before you.
Sunjata's mother's name was Sukulung Konte.
Sukulung Konte,
Her father was Sankarang Madiba Konte.
Sankarang Madiba Konte,
He was a great king.
That king,
Sankarang Madiba Konte, was descended from
    Khulubu Konte;

Khulubu Konte,
It was he who begat Khulubu Khalaba Konte.
Sankarang Khulubu Konte and Khulubu Khalaba
    Konte –
It was Dala Kumbukamba who was the father of Dala
    Jiibaa Minna;
Dala Jiibaa Minna was the father of Kasawura Konte;
It was Kasawura Konte who was the ancestor of
    Sunjata,
As I have heard it.

In the reign of Dugu and Bala, Faabaga and Taulajo,
Sunjata's mother, Sukulung Konte, was that king's
    sister.
Sunjata's father,
Naareng Makhang Konnate,
In their section of the town,
He fathered twelve sons.
Naareng Sira
Was the father of Naareng Makhang,
Naareng Makhang was the father of Makhang Konnate,
Makhang Konnate was the father of Makhang Sunjata.
Before Sunjata was born,
As I have heard it from the traditional narrators,
His mother had had twenty pregnancies by his father –
Forty sons.
At that time Mansa Farang Tunkara
Was reigning, the ancestor of the Tunkaras,
But he was not within the town of Manding.
It was the head of the smiths, Susu Sumanguru
    Baamagana,

Who was at that time reigning in Manding.
There were twelve sections in Manding;
The Jaanes had a section there,
The Kommas had a section there,
The Tures had a section there,
The Siises had a section there.
All of these were within the town of Manding,
But they were not in control of the town,
They did not seek the kingship;
They had their Islamic faith.
Dugu and Bala,
Faabaga and Taulajo,
Supreme horseman whom none surpasses.
Susu Sumanguru Baamagana, the ancestor of the
    smiths,
He it was who was at that time the king of Manding.
They used to quarry iron ore and smelt it and make
    iron from it and forge it.
They made guns with it,
And they made bullets with it.
He used to make his own gunpowder;
He it was who was in control of the town of Manding.
In his time
A tall, slender baobab tree grew within the town of
    Manding.
This little baobab tree was round; it grew up,
And produced a single fruit.
When you say 'one single fruit',
That means that it produced one fruit.
As to that fruit, all the marabouts declared it,
All the diviners by cowries declared it,

All the diviners by stones declared it,
The diviners by sand declared it,
They predicted that whoever swallowed a single seed
    of the fruit of that baobab
Would be in control of the town of Manding for sixty
    years.
Before Sunjata was born,
The forty sons whom his father had begot
Had perished in the Prophet's war at Haibara.
Then in the days of the Prophet Muhammad,
That too was the time of Sunjata's father.
Those forty sons became soldiers of the Prophet;
They went to the war at Haibara, where they perished.
It befell that the Prophet
Sent Sorakhata Bunjafar to Sunjata's father,
With the message, 'You must give me soldiers;
I am going to wage war upon the infidels at Haibara.'
Sorakhata came and stood by Sunjata's father
And said to him, 'The handsome Slave of God says that
    you must give him soldiers;
They are going to fight at Haibara.'
Sunjata's father called Sunjata's mother, Sukulung
    Konte,
And he said to her,
'The Messenger of God has sent this man here;
He says that I must give him fighting men,
Because he is going to wage war at Haibara.'
He summoned his wife to speak.
His wife said to him, 'From the time that I married you
Up to this year – how many years does that make?'
He told her the number of years.

She said to him, 'Have I ever gainsaid you?'
He answered, 'No.'
'Have I ever refused you anything?'
He answered, 'No.'
She said to him, 'I serve you,
I serve God,
When you say what should be done,
Am I to argue with you about it?'
He gave his forty sons to Sorakhata Bunjafar,
And they went off to the Prophet's war at Haibara,
    where they perished.
When God's Messenger withdrew from the Haibara
    war,
Then the war was over.
Sukulung Kutuma,
And Sukulung Yammaru,
Naareng Makhang Konnate,
Cats on the shoulder,
Simbong and Jata are at Naarena.
When the Prophet had returned home he summoned
    Sorakhata
And said to him, 'Sorakhata, go and tell Makhang
    Konnate
That his forty sons have perished.'
At that time Sunjata's mother was old;
For a long time she and Sunjata's father had not lived
    in the same house,
For a period of some twelve years in fact.
They just cooked lunch for the two of them,
They used to eat and sit together in the same place and
    converse with each other,

But his mother had passed the age
Of going into the husband's house.
This tune which I am playing
Is one which was played to Sunjata in Manding.
This tune was played to Faa Koli Kumba and Faa Koli
    Daaba.
He was a fierce warrior of Sunjata's.
He was descended from the ancestor of the Sooras,
Kiliya Musa and Nooya Musa,
Bula Wuruwuru and Bula Wanjaga,
Futu Yokhobila and Sina Yokhobila,
Bumba Yokhobila;
He had a spear
Which was called *Tuluku Muluku,*
*One place where it enters, nine places where blood comes
    forth.*
If it pierced your body in one place,
Blood would issue forth in nine places.
That is why he was called Soora: Piercer;
In the eastern dialect they call him 'Soora'.
Sorakhata arrived,
He came and stood by Makhang Konnate,
And he said to him, '*Dugu and Bala,*
Faabaga and Taulajo,
Supreme horseman whom none surpasses,
Wuruwarang Kaba,
Dala Kumbukamba,
And Dala Jiibaa Minna,
Kasawura Konte,
Dugu and Bala,
Faabaga and Taulajo,

Supreme horseman whom none surpasses.'
He said, *'Sukulung Kutuma,*
And Sukulung Yammaru,
Naareng Makhang Konnate,
Cats on the shoulder,
Simbong and Jata are at Naarena.'
He said to him, 'God's Messenger declared that I
    should tell you
That all your forty sons have perished at Haibara.'
Makhang Konnate leapt up and shouted, 'Praise be to
    God, Master of the worlds,
I shall give thanks to the Lord who created me;
Even though I myself have done no service for God
    which would take me to Paradise
Those forty sons of mine,
Whom I got in honourable wedlock –
I believe that the Holy War in which they died
Will save my wife and myself in the next world.'
Sorakhata returned
And delivered this report to God's Messenger;
God's Messenger went into retreat at night
And performed twelve *rak'a*.
He begged God
To send down good fortune upon Sunjata's mother
    and father,
And to provide them with means of support.
After that, God in His omnipotence
Returned Sunjata's mother to what she had been as a
    young woman.
Her flesh did not change,
But she reverted to a fourteen-year-old girl.

She approached Sunjata's father
And she became pregnant with Sunjata.
At that time Sunjata's sister was there;
She was called Nene Faamaga.
At that time the leader of the smiths was king of
    Manding.
That baobab tree which grew within the town of
    Manding
Had had dry wood piled up round it.
It was announced that when the fruit of the baobab
    fell,
One person from each section of the town should get
    some and eat it,
Since, as to that baobab tree,
The marabouts had declared,
And the diviners by cowries had likewise declared,
That whoever ate one seed of that baobab tree
Would be in control of the town of Manding for sixty
    years.
After Sunjata's mother had become pregnant,
In the seventh month of her pregnancy, Sunjata's
    father died.
Only she and Sunjata's sister were left.
His mother was left with nothing
Except a cow and its calf and one cat and one dog.
That cow was in the herd,
Together with its one calf;
When they had fetched the milk,
Sunjata's mother used to curdle it,
And when she had exchanged the curdled milk for
    millet,

She would pound the millet,
She would put the flour in a steamer,
And that, with the little drop of milk left over,
Was what she and Sunjata's sister lived on.
Sunjata was not yet born.

Kiliya Musa and Nooya Musa,
Bula Wuruwuru and Bula Wanjaga,
Futu Yokhobila, Sina Yokhobila, Karata Kobila,
Bagala Nyankang Musa and Fitaga Musa,
Bula Banna Jajura.
The drums which were used to summon an assembly
    sounded for his grandfather,
Great Bagadugu and Ginate,
Great Hanjulu and Hanunayanga,
They say that Faa Koli Kumba had a spear and a bow,
Faa Koli Daaba,
At that time he was in Manding.
It was Jinna Musa who was his father.

Of Sunjata's mother,
People used to say,
'Is this woman pregnant,
Or is she ill, or has she been poisoned?'
After it had happened,
That Sunjata's mother had become pregnant,
When she had been pregnant for one year,
Susu Sumanguru Baamagana's diviners by stones said
    to him,
'The child who will destroy your kingship
Has been conceived within Manding.'

Sumanguru gathered together all the women of the
    town of Manding,
And for seven years
He kept them within a walled town.
A man and a woman did not lie on the same bed,
A man and a woman did not come near each other.
As for those women who did become pregnant,
If they gave birth to a child and that child was a male,
Its throat was cut – for seven years.
When it became known that Sunjata had been
    conceived,
The griots composed this song:
Ah, it is of Jata that I speak, great stock,
Simbong, it is of Jata that I speak, great stock destined for
    high office.
In those seven years,
Any woman who became pregnant in Manding
Was taken inside that walled town,
And this went on for fourteen years.
For fourteen years
Sunjata's mother was pregnant with him,
But the diviners by stones foretold it,
The diviners by cowries foretold it;
They told Susu Sumanguru Baamagana,
'The child who will destroy your kingship
Has already been conceived.'
Sukulung Kutuma,
And Sukulung Yammaru,
Naareng Makhang Konnate,
Cats on the shoulder,
Simbong and Jata are at Naarena.

As to Sunjata's reputed running away,
The griots made a fine name out of it.
Susu Sumanguru Baamagana went to the leader of the
    Siises,
And sent him into retreat for forty days.
This child who was to destroy his kingship –
Had he been born yet?
Or had he not?
Was he in Manding?
These were the questions he must answer.
He must devise some strategy
So that he can work magic against the child and so be
    able to kill him.
The leader of the Siises went into retreat;
He came out,
And he found Susu Sumanguru Baamagana –
Cut and Sirimang,
It is forging and the left hand,
Senegalese coucal and swallow,
Cut iron with iron,
What gives iron its excellence,
Big kuku *tree and big silk-cotton tree,*
Fari and Kaunju –
He was sitting.
He told Sumanguru, 'I went into retreat
For forty days;
I saw the seven layers of the sky,
Right to where they finish;
I saw the seven layers of the earth,
Right to where they finish;
I saw a black thing in a pond;

By the grace of God,
The creature which comes and gives me information in
    the night
Came and stood beside me and said,
"Allahu aharu rajaku fa mang kaana kaafa,
Ming muusi, janafang kumfai kuna."
God declares that by his grace,
Whomsoever he has created king,
He has made his own likeness,
And nothing will be able to injure that person.
Those things which you must enjoy,
Enjoy them now, before this child is born,
For after he is born,
You will be powerless against him.
If you do not believe that,
You should release two white cocks within your
    compound,
And name one of them after yourself,
And one after this child.
Since you do not know his name,
You must mark it in some way;
You must fashion pure gold
And put it on your namesake's leg,
And you must fashion pure silver
And put it on the leg of the child's one.'
Sukulung Kutuma
And Sukulung Yammaru,
Naareng Makhang Konnate,
Cats on the shoulder,
Simbong and Jata are at Naarena.
In Sunjata's day a griot did not have to fetch water,

To say nothing of farming and collecting firewood.
Father World has changed, changed.
Almighty God, my thoughts here go to
Makhang Sunjata, a wonderful episode.
Sumanguru kept those two white cocks in his
    compound.
A day came
When Susu Sumanguru Baamagana
And his griots were sitting,
Along with his smiths
And his attendants.
At that time Bala Faasigi Kuyate belonged to Susu
    Sumanguru Baamagana.
A marabout arrived;
Sumanguru was sitting;
Bala Faasigi Kuyate said,
'Cut and Sirimang,
It is forging and the left hand,
Senegalese coucal and swallow,
Cut iron with iron,
What makes iron valuable,
Big kuku tree and big silk-cotton tree,
Fari and Kaunju.'
The chicken named after Sunjata crowed.
When the one named after Sunjata crowed,
The one named after Susu Sumanguru Baamagana also
    crowed.
When the one named after Sumanguru crowed,
The one named after Sunjata attacked it.
They seized hold of each other,
And fought,

And fought,
And fought,
Till the one named after Sumanguru turned tail
And ran under the leg of Sumanguru's chair.
The one named after Sunjata seized it by the comb
And pulled it out
And shook it;
It opened its mouth,
And saliva dribbled out.
The griot, Bala Faasigi Kuyate, was sitting.
Susu Sumanguru Baamagana ordered,
'Go and catch that chicken and destroy it;
Don't let it die a natural death.'
They seized it and slaughtered it.
The marabout was sitting;
He said, 'Susu Sumanguru Baamagana,
I went into retreat –
Is this the votive offering which I prescribed for you?'
Sumanguru said, 'Yes.'
The marabout asked, 'Did you see what one chicken
      did to the other?
If you touch this child,
That is what he will do to you.'
(As you may know, the members of the Kante family
      do not eat white chicken,
And the reason for this is
That when Sunjata and Susu Sumanguru met,
It was a white chicken which killed the latter.
As to the white chicken which killed him,
They took the spur of a white cock
And they put gold dust and silver dust inside it,

And that is what they eventually killed Susu
    Sumanguru Baamagana with.
After Sunjata had captured them,
He changed the smiths' surname;
He made their surname Kante.
As regards all those in Manding,
That is the reason that the members of the Kante
    family do not eat white chicken.
I shall come to that in due course,
And I shall tell you about that when I come to it.)
....

Susu Sumanguru Baamagana was perplexed;
He lay down for the night.
All this time Sunjata's mother was pregnant with him.
All this took place in those twelve years.
Sumanguru went to the leader of the Jaanes
And took him to his compound,
Where they sat together;
He said, 'Bala Faasigi Kuyate!',
And the latter answered;
Sumanguru went on, 'I summoned the leader of the
    Siises,
And told him to divine by dreams
And to divine also by other techniques
So that he could devise some stratagem against the
    child who, it is said,
Will be born in Manding,
And who will destroy my kingship –
Some stratagem so that he could work against the child
    on my behalf
And destroy him for me

Before he comes to anything.
He went into retreat;
After forty days he came out.
He prescribed two white chickens as a votive offering;
I kept those two white chickens in my compound.
Of those two white chickens,
The one named after the child killed the one named
    after me.
I have called upon the leader of the Jaanes
To work for me,
And to investigate how things stand for me,
And to see if he can do anything.'
Sukulung Kutuma
And Sukulung Yammaru,
Naareng Makhang Konnate,
Cats on the shoulder,
Simbong and Jata are at Naarena.
The leader of the Jaanes replied, 'All right, I have
    heard.'
He too went off;
He went into retreat;
After forty days he came out.
That is why,
Among us black people,
A white cock is prescribed as a votive offering,
For every boy.
Afterwards, when you grow up and build your own
    compound,
A white ram is prescribed as an offering by you.
As to the origin of this custom,
This is how it came about.

He too went into retreat;
After forty days he came out.
He came and said to Susu Sumanguru Baamagana,
'I have seen the seven layers of the sky,
Right to where they end;
I have seen the seven layers of the earth,
Right to where they end;
The creature which often stands beside me
Came and stood beside me,
A spirit in human form,
And it said to me, "Hata nuta
Muslama utiya rusululai
Wollahi alamu."
It said that a created thing will not know God.
God declared that he had ordained this and it could not
    be altered.
But if you do not believe it,
You must give two white rams as a votive offering.
You must name one of them after yourself,
And the name of the person whom you fear,
That person whom God will make manifest,
His name must you give to the other ram.
You must watch those two white rams,
Because what happens with them
Will, if you touch this child,
Happen also with the two of you.'
All this time Sunjata's mother was pregnant with him.
He had a sister, Nene Faamaga,
Who was in love with a spirit king.
That spirit king
Lived in a hill called Yura.

The spirit king's name was Manga.
You must have noticed among the griots
A tune which they play called 'Manga Yira';
It is not strictly 'Manga Yira', it is 'Manga Yura'.
Every Monday night
Sunjata's sister would go and sleep with that spirit king,
    Manga Yura.
In the Yalunka language, when you hear the word
    mangga,
That means 'king';
Yura means 'hill'.
That hill, Yura, stood on the outskirts of the town of
    Manding.
Every Monday night
Nene Faamaga would go and sleep with the spirit king
    there.
Every Friday night
She would go and sleep with the spirit king,
And he would say to her, 'This pregnancy of your
    mother's –
The child she is to bear will become a king;
His name will be Sunjata.'
The leader of the Jaanes
Prescribed these two white rams
For Susu Sumanguru Baamagana.
Cut and Sirimang,
It is forging and the left hand,
Senegalese coucal and swallow,
Cut iron with iron,
What makes iron valuable,
Big kuku tree and big silk-cotton tree,

Fari and Kaunju;
The smith who brings out the koma *masquerader is leading*
    the smiths,
Fataga Magaso is leading the smiths.
Don't you see,
Susu Sumanguru Baamagana is cold;
Their day is past.
Sumanguru kept the two white rams in his compound.
He fashioned pure silver
And attached it to the leg of the one named after
    himself;
He intended to change matters.
He fashioned pure gold
And attached it to the one he had named after Sunjata.
Since he did not know Sunjata's name
He said, 'The person whom God is to create,
Is he not yet born?
Is he in this town?
Is he in his mother's womb?
Is he a spirit?
If it be God's will,
It is that child who will destroy my reign;
It is after him that I name this ram.'
He put the pure gold on that one.
Those two white rams were together for some time,
Then a day came,
Susu Sumanguru Baamagana –
It was the evening before Friday;
Thursday was nearly over and the evening before
    Friday had begun,
When dawn broke it would be Friday –

Susu Sumanguru Baamagana and his attendants were
    sitting;
The sheep appeared,
With the two white rams among them;
The one named after Sunjata mounted a ewe
And was about to couple with it;
The one named after Sumanguru took a few steps
    backwards
And butted the one named after Sunjata.
The latter left the ewe
And faced the other ram.
They butted each other,
And butted each other,
And butted each other,
Susu Sumanguru Baamagana was sitting
With his griots
And his attendants.
The ram named after Susu Sumanguru Baamagana
Pulled back a little way,
Sunjata's namesake did likewise;
As they crashed into each other,
One of the horns of Susu Sumanguru Baamagana's
    namesake snapped.
Sunjata's namesake pulled back a little way,
Then came crashing into the other ram,
Which fell to the ground.
The attendants fell upon it and slaughtered it.
Sumanguru was perplexed;
He went to the leader of the Jaanes,
And told him what had happened.
The leader of the Jaanes said to him,

'I am not God,
But since I began serving God,
Since I first knew my right hand from my left,
On any occasion when someone gave me work to do,
I went into retreat,
And what I saw, I saw;
That is what I have seen in this instance.
That is what the Lord has revealed to me.
He declares that he is God and that no one can know
    him.
He has ordained this kingship and it cannot be
    altered.
Therefore enjoy such luck as you are going to enjoy
Before this child appears.'
....

Sumanguru went to the leader of the Kommas.
When he had summoned the leader of the Kommas,
The latter came.
Susu Sumanguru Baamagana said to him,
'Leader of the Kommas,
I summoned the leader of the Siises
And I set him to work on this matter;
He went into retreat,
And after forty days he came out,
And he prescribed a chicken as a votive offering – two
    white chickens.
I kept two white chickens in my compound,
And when I did that,
The namesake of the person I am afraid of
Killed my namesake.
Then I went to the leader of the Jaanes,

And I set him to work on this same matter.
He too went into retreat,
For forty days;
He prescribed two rams for me as an offering.
The child's namesake killed my namesake.
I have come to you, leader of the Kommas,
To help me,
So that, as far as this child is concerned,
Even if I cannot kill him,
At least I may remain king,
And no one may drive me from the kingship.'
The leader of the Kommas went into retreat, then
      came out,
And he said to Sumanguru, 'Until three years have
      elapsed I shall not be able to work against him.'
Within that time Sunjata was born;
He was a male child.
His mother went to the wash-place
And there she dug a hole
Into which she put Sunjata.
Then she put a steamer on top of him
So that he could breathe,
For she was afraid.
The diviners by stones were telling Susu Sumanguru
      Baamagana,
'A woman is about to give birth
Either this month or next,
And it is a son that she will bear;
That is the child who will destroy your reign.'
Sunjata's mother went to the wash-place
And dug a deep hole

Into which she put the infant Sunjata;
Then she put a steamer on top of him.
When dawn broke
She would go and suckle him,
Then replace the steamer on top of him,
And go into town
In search of work.
When she had pounded millet for someone,
She used to bring the hard pieces of millet
And pound them
And put them in a steamer like flour.
Sunjata's sister, Nene Faamaga,
And her spirit king were lovers.
They remained like that for three years.
Then the leader of the Kommas came
To Susu Sumanguru Baamagana;
He found Bala Faasigi Kuyate sitting,
And Bala said,
'Cut and Sirimang,
It is forging and the left hand,
Senegalese coucal and swallow,
Cut iron with iron,
What makes iron valuable,
Big kuku tree and big silk-cotton tree,
Fari and Kaunju.'
After that had taken place,
The leader of the Kommas said,
'The three years are now completed;
I am going into retreat,
For forty days.
When I come out,

The work which I must do,
I shall do.'
He went into retreat.
When he came out,
He came and found Susu Sumanguru Baamagana
    sitting.
Bala Faasigi Kuyate was sitting;
He jumped to his feet and shouted praises:
'*Great Jaane, Muslim of Manding,*
Great Ture, Muslim of Manding,
Great Siise, Muslim of Manding,
Great Komma, Muslim of Manding,
Great Berete, Muslim of Manding,
Saint of saints.'
The leader of the Kommas said, 'Susu Sumanguru
    Baamagana,
I have served God
For forty days,
And from what I have seen,
One must pray
That you remain king till your death,
But you are powerless to prevent this child from
    becoming king.
God has written that down and it cannot be altered.
You must help me with a live porcupine,
One which has not died,
Which has not been shot, but which has been caught
    and brought here,
And from which a quill has been plucked.
I shall make a divinatory pattern with it,
And on the skull

Of a child who has been born but died before it was
    named
I shall make a charm.'
Bala Faasigi Kuyate sought those things;
The leader of the Kommas told him, 'I did not say a
    child who has been seized and had its throat cut;
I said that a child should be born,
But before it was named,
God should come and take its life.
I shall make a charm upon its skull,
And you must bury it in your house.
I shall make two patterns,
And put one of them on a stone;
You must find a white stone
And give it to me, along with a piece of paper.
I shall make these two patterns on them
And I shall take them and throw them into the Niger.
When I have thrown them into the river,
The person associated with the one which sinks will die
Between now and your war.'
Four years passed quietly;
They did not get a baby for that purpose.
In the fourth year,
A baby was obtained.
It had died, and they got its skull.
That skull
They took to the leader of the Kommas;
Then they went and caught a live porcupine and
    brought it to him;
He plucked out a quill.
They dug up a white stone,

And they chipped it to the shape of a writing board,
And took it to him.
They brought him paper;
He went into retreat.
He told Sumanguru, 'On Monday night
You must get into a canoe,
And go and throw this into the Niger,
And you must make a vow upon it;
You must declare that
The person of whom you are afraid,
The person who is to be born in Manding,
And who is to destroy your reign,
That his name is on this stone,
And that your name, Susu Sumanguru Baamagana,
Is on the piece of paper.
You must throw them into the Niger;
If one of them sinks,
Then when you and he join battle,
The person associated with that one will perish.'
Sukulung Kutuma,
And Sukulung Yammaru,
Naareng Makhang Konnate,
Cats on the shoulder,
Simbong and Jata are at Naarena;
Makhang Sunjata's alleged running away,
The griots made a fine name of it.
In Sunjata's day in wondrous Manding
A griot did not have to carry water,
To say nothing of farming and fetching firewood.
Father World has changed, changed.
They sat till midnight on Monday.

Banna Kanute

Cut and Sirimang,
It is forging and the left hand,
Senegalese coucal and swallow,
Cut iron with iron,
And what makes iron valuable,
Big kuku tree and big silk-cotton tree,
Fari and Kaunju.
He and his griot rose up,
Bala Faasigi Kuyate,
And got into a canoe, along with a man to paddle it;
They threw the stone and the piece of paper into the
    river.
Sir, it is of Jata that I speak, great stock,
Simbong, it is of Jata that I speak, great stock.
Prince of the Keita line,
Sukulung Kutuma,
And Sukulung Yammaru,
Naareng Makhang Konnate,
Cats on the shoulder,
Simbong and Jata are at Naarena.
He was the son of Khulubu Konte,
Khulubu Konte was the son of Khulubu Khalaba Konte,
Sankarang nine boils,
And six manyang daa.
Faa Ganda used to kill his in-law on Monday,
And by the next Monday Faa Ganda was king.
Sankarang Daminya Konte,
It was he who begat Sukulung Konte,
It was Sukulung Konte who bore Makhang Sunjata.
At that time Sunjata was sitting in the hole;
He was twelve years old,

But he could not crawl,
Much less stand up,
Much less walk.
He was just sitting near the house;
He was sitting in his mother's washing enclosure.
When that happened,
They went on till they reached the middle of the Niger.
Susu Sumanguru Baamagana declared,
'I kept two white chickens in my compound,
The leader of the Siises told me
That I should do so as a votive offering.
I kept these two white chickens in my compound,
And the child's namesake killed my namesake.
I kept two white rams in my compound;
The leader of the Jaanes told me
That I should do that as an offering.
The child's namesake killed my namesake.
The leader of the Kommas has prepared
A stone and a piece of paper
And said to throw them into the Niger.
When I throw them in,
If one of them goes down into the water,
Then the person associated with it is doomed.'
He threw the stone and piece of paper into the water;
The paper spun round and round and then settled at
        the bottom of the river and the stone floated.
From this event the griots say:
Tuu taro jii,
Nii ke laa bere la jii kang,
Bere jee ni wuya.
That is one of Sunjata's songs;

I shall come to that in the course of my narration.
Don't you know, Makhang Sunjata is cold;
He was the son of Sukulung Kutuma
And Sukulung Yammaru.
Naareng Makhang Konnate,
Cats on the shoulder,
Simbong and Jata are at Naarena.
Both he and Faa Koli Kumba-and-
Faa Koli Daaba distinguished themselves in Manding.
He came from Woliwolinki,
Great Tambaki, Magasugu Gandana,
Kutu Yokhobila,
Sina Yokhobila,
Karata Kobila,
Great Bahala Nangang Musa,
And Fitaga Musa,
Bula Banna Gajola.
The royal drums sounded for his grandfather.
Great Bagadugu and Ginate,
Great Hanjulu and Hamina Yanga.
(The last two lines refer to Jinna Musa;
Jinna Musa was the father of Faa Koli Kumba,
And the father of Faa Koli Daaba.
Faa Koli Kumba and Faa Koli Daaba
Left Manding with a spear and a bow;
He was Sunjata's military commander.)
Sumanguru returned,
He came home,
And summoned the leader of the Kommas.
The latter said to Sumanguru,
'What you have to enjoy,

You must enjoy before this boy grows up.'
Sunjata was then thirteen years old.
Sumanguru summoned the leader of the Tures,
And he told him, 'I want
You to help me.
This child who wishes to destroy my reign –
I no longer aspire to destroy his kingship,
But you must pray for me
That before I die
No one will remove me from the kingship,
But that I may remain king.'
The leader of the Serahuli, Mansa Farang Tunkara,
Was at that time king in his own territory.
Sunjata was then fourteen years old.
That year Manding had to hold a circumcision
    ceremony,
But at that time Sunjata
Could not crawl,
Much less stand up,
Much less walk.
The baobab tree which was in the middle of the town
    of Manding
Had produced a single fruit, high up;
All Manding was guarding that baobab tree –
The Komma section provided a hundred men,
The Jaane section provided a hundred men,
The Ture section provided a hundred men,
The Siise section provided a hundred men,
The Berete section provided a hundred men,
Susu Sumanguru Baamagana's section provided a
    hundred men;

They placed dry wood all round that baobab tree,
And they guarded it
Night and day, all the time,
So that when the baobab fruit fell no one else might
  swallow the seed
But that Susu Sumanguru Baamagana might get it.
They appointed a day for the circumcision ceremony,
And they proclaimed that on the fourteenth day of the
  next month
They would hold a circumcision ceremony in Manding.
Every section was to enter a hundred boys;
Every boy who was to go into the bush
Would mount a horse,
With a gun in his hand
And wearing a sword.
When the smith had circumcised you,
You fired your gun and mounted your horse.
Sunjata called his mother,
And his sister Nene Faamaga,
And he said, 'Mother,'
And she replied, 'Yes.'
He said to her, 'My brothers will never go to
  circumcision
And leave me here.'
His mother wept,
And she said to him, 'Sunjata,
I give thanks to God this day.
Forty sons have I borne,
And all have died in the Prophet's war at Haibara.
You have no father,
You have no uncle,

You have no older brother,
You have no step-mother,
You have no aunt,
You have no slave,
I have no possessions,
Except this one sister of yours,
Nene Faamaga.'
. . . .

Sunjata's mother wept;
He said to her, 'Mother, my brothers will never go to
    circumcision
And leave me here.'
Sunjata's mother, Sukulung Konte, took the road;
She went and stood by the leader of the smiths, Susu
    Sumanguru Baamagana,
And she addressed him, 'Susu Sumanguru Baamagana,
I have come to you.'
He said, 'Why?'
She answered, 'My child who is unable to walk
Says that when the circumcision ceremony is held he
    too will go to circumcision';
She added, 'I have no slave,
And he has no uncle.'
When she had spoken these words
To Susu Sumanguru Baamagana,
He said to her,
'And what do you say that I should do?'
She answered, 'I say that you should help me
So that my son may rise up and walk.'
Sumanguru said, 'All right.'
The leader of the griots, Bala Faasigi Kuyate, stood up,

And he said, 'Cut and Sirimang,
It is forging and the left hand,
Senegalese coucal and swallow,
Cut iron with iron,
What makes iron valuable,
Big kuku tree and big silk-cotton tree,
Fari and Kaunju.'
He continued, 'Defender of orphans,
Forge iron and give it to him so that he may rise up.'
As you know, when someone's leg is broken,
The smiths fashion a staff which they give to him,
And he puts it under his arm –
Two such staffs.
Susu Sumanguru Baamagana
Sounded the drums and the young smiths assembled;
He ordered them to quarry ore and fashion it.
They quarried iron ore and smelted it,
And they fashioned it into a very long rod.
They cut it in two
And they bent it.
Three full-grown men took each rod and brought it.
They found Sunjata sitting in his mother's doorway –
Sukulung Kutuma,
And Sukulung Yammaru,
Naareng Makhang Konnate,
Cats on the shoulder,
Simbong and Jata are at Naarena,
Bone-breaking Lion,
Tie Manding Simbara and untie Simbara.
They laid the rods down beside him, and he laughed,
And said, 'Mother,

These rods cannot accomplish my rising up.
When the day comes for me to rise up,'
He said, 'That day I shall rise up.
But I must tell you this,
My brothers will not go to circumcision and leave me
    here.'
When he put his weight on the rods,
He pressed his hands on the ground, and the rods
    buckled;
He grabbed them, he picked them up and flung them
    away from where he was sitting.
The people were afraid, and they went and told Susu
    Sumanguru Baamagana.
That day he summoned diviners by stones,
He summoned diviners by cowries,
He summoned diviners by sand,
He summoned Muslim diviners,
And they looked into matters concerning Sunjata.
They told Sumanguru, 'The child who will destroy
    your kingship – this is he.'
Sumanguru said, 'This one who is sitting like that,
    unable to move?'
They said, 'Yes.'
Sumanguru said, 'In that case I shall employ a
    stratagem against him before he gets up and stands
    on his feet.'
He went to the owners of fetishes,
And to the owners of medicine powders,
And to the *korte* men,
And there was much coming and going between him
    and them.

They tried everything against Sunjata;
He was sitting, unable to move,
Till the day when they had to hold the circumcision
    ceremony.
The uncircumcised boys went into the bush to pick
    baobab leaves
And they dried them for their mothers,
Who pounded those baobab leaves and winnowed
    them and set down the powder.
The Lion was sitting at his mother's doorway;
He did not budge
Until the day before the boys were to go into
    circumcision,
The day when women were putting into steamers the
    couscous
Which the circumcision candidates would eat before
    going into the bush;
Sunjata's mother got up.
When she went into town,
Whenever she begged anyone for baobab leaf to put on
    Sunjata's couscous,
That person would say to her, 'You don't know what
    you are saying.
My child who is in good health –
The baobab leaf which he went and picked for me
He brought here
And dried,
And I pounded it,
And I shall put it on his couscous.
I shall not put any of my child's baobab leaf on your
    child's couscous,

That child of yours who is deformed and shapeless
And a cripple,
Who has no mother,
No father,
No uncle,
No brother,
No slave,
No horse –
How is he going to go to circumcision?
Don't make fun of me.'
His mother came home in tears in the evening.
Sunjata said to her, 'Mother, what are you crying
about?'
She said to him, 'I went to look for baobab leaf in
town;
I intended to put it on the food you would eat the
evening before you went to circumcision.
Whoever I asked for baobab leaf
Refused me
And said that my son who is deformed and shapeless –
Did I think that they would take some of their baobab
leaf
And give to me to put on his food?'
Sunjata laughed,
And he said to his mother, 'Today you will have no
more worries about baobab leaf.'
Sukulung Kutuma,
And Sukulung Yammaru,
Naareng Makhang Konnate,
Cats on the shoulder,
Simbong and Jata are at Naarena,

Bone breaking Lion,
Tie Simbara and untie Simbara,
He came from Khulubu Konte
And Khulubu Khalaba Konte,
Sankarang's six boils
And six manyang daa.
Faa Ganda killed his in-law on Monday,
The following Monday, Faa Ganda was king.
He came from Sankarang Daminya Konte.

Sunjata arose in this fashion:
He grasped the eaves of his mother's house,
He arose and stood up,
He laid his hands upon the middle of the roof, high up;
He called upon God three times,
And he stretched out his hand.
The baobab tree which stood in the middle of the town
    of Manding,
And which slaves were guarding,
And armed men were guarding –
Sunjata seized that baobab tree and twisted it,
And laid it at his mother's doorway.
He split open the baobab fruit and swallowed it.
To his mother he said, 'Here is some baobab leaf!'
The fourteen drums of Manding all sounded.
Susu Sumanguru Baamagana and his griots all rose to
    their feet,
Along with his attendants,
And they came and found Sunjata standing with his
    hand resting upon the roof of the house.
His mother was weeping,

His sister was weeping;
He said to his mother, 'Pick some baobab leaf!'
Susu Sumanguru Baamagana demanded, 'Who felled
    this baobab tree?'
Sunjata answered, 'I, Sunjata.'
Sumanguru asked, 'Why did you fell the baobab tree?'
Sunjata replied, 'My mother went to look for baobab
    leaf in the town,
To put on the food I was to eat before going into
    circumcision,
But she got no baobab leaf.
She was told to order me to go and pick baobab leaf;
That is why I felled this baobab tree.'
Sumanguru demanded, 'What about the baobab fruit?'
Sunjata replied, 'I have swallowed it.'
Sumanguru asked, 'Why did you swallow the fruit of
    this baobab tree?'
Sunjata answered, 'Now you have come to the point,
Now you have come to it,'
(In the eastern dialect, 'I bara naa kuma di').
Sunjata continued, 'I don't want it,
I don't want anything in Manding,
Except a son,
An older sister,
A wife,
An attendant,
A griot,
And a smith.'
Susu Sumanguru Baamagana said, 'What did you say?'
Sunjata answered, 'That is what I said.'
Sumanguru said, 'Ni wadi,'

That is, 'We are against each other.'
Susu Sumanguru Baamagana turned his back on Sunjata.
His griot proclaimed: *'Cut and Sirimang,*
It is forging and the left hand,
Senegalese coucal and swallow,
Cut iron with iron,
What makes iron valuable,
Big kuku *tree and big silk-cotton tree,*
Fari and Kaunju.'
He said, 'The smith who brings out the koma *masquerader*
    is in the forefront of the smiths,
Fataga Magaso is in the forefront of the smiths,
A smith of pure blood is in the forefront of the smiths.'
Sumanguru sounded the drum which summoned the
    people to assembly,
He called together all the smiths
Who were to perform the circumcision,
And he addressed them: 'Tomorrow when the
    circumcision candidates go into the bush,
The boy who is called Sunjata –
You must cut off his genitals completely and remove
    them so that he dies.'
There was one elderly man there who said, 'Ah, that is
    not at all a simple matter,
Because if we are to do that,
With four hundred and one candidates
One does not know which is Sunjata;
The smiths who are coming
Will not be able to distinguish Sunjata from the others;
What if they were to do that to someone else's child?
We would murder each other in the bush.'

'That is true,' the others said;
'In that case let us load a gun with powder
And put one metal bullet in it
And give it to someone,
Because when they have circumcised a candidate he
        fires a gun;
When Sunjata fires his gun,
The person with the gun with the bullet in it will shoot
        him and he will die.'
One man declared, 'That also is not feasible,
Because if we give this gun to someone and he fires it,
What happens if the bullet goes right through Sunjata
        and comes out and then enters the body of
        someone else's child?
Or what if the bullet misses Sunjata and goes and kills
        someone else?
There would certainly be fighting then.'
They said, 'Let's leave him.'
Then Susu Sumanguru Baamagana said,
'Let's leave him; let him go into the bush;
Before he comes out of the circumcision area
I shall think of something that will enable me to kill
        him.'
Sukulung Kutuma,
And Sukulung Yammaru,
Naareng Makhang Konnate
Don't you know that death spares no one at all,
Don't you realize that Makhang Sunjata is cold;
Their day is past.
Sunjata is descended from whom and whom?
He is descended from Sukulung Kutuma

And Sukulung Yammaru.
Naareng Makhang Konnate,
Cats on the shoulder,
Simbong and Jata are at Naarena.
His mother's side is
Dugu and Bala,
Faabaga and Taulajo,
Supreme horseman whom none surpasses,
Wuruwarang Kaba,
Dala Kumbukamba,
And Dala Jiibaa Minna,
Kasawura Konte.
Sukulung Konte was descended from Sukulung Kuma,
The latter was descended from Khulubu Konte,
Khulubu Konte was the father of Khulubu Khalaba Konte,
*Khulubu Khalaba Konte was the father of Sankarang
    Daminya Konte,*
*Sankarang Daminya Konte was the father of Faabaga and
    Taulajo,*
*Faabaga and Taulajo was the father of Sankarang Madiba
    Konte,*
*Sankarang Madiba Konte was the father of Sukulung
    Kutuma Konte,*
And she it was who bore Sunjata.
Sunjata and the other boys went to the circumcision
    area.
While they were there,
Susu Sumanguru Baamagana summoned the head of
    the Ture family,
And said to him, 'I set the head of the Jaane family to
    work

To find a countermeasure to this child, but we did not
    find one.
He prescribed two white rams for me as a votive
    offering;
The child's namesake killed my namesake.
I set the head of the Siise family to work
To find a countermeasure to this child, but we did not
    find one.
He prescribed two white chickens for me as an
    offering;
The child's namesake killed my namesake.
I set the head of the Komma family to work
Against this child.
He prepared stone and paper,
And I took them to the Niger;
The one with my name attached to it sank,
The one with the child's name attached to it came to
    the surface.
Head of the Ture family and head of the Berete family,'
    he said,
'I have given you the task of dealing with this child.
He is in the circumcision area.
He is in the bush,
And before he leaves it,
You must think of some means of destroying him.'
In Mandinka, that means
He gave the task of dealing with the child to these two
    men,
Great Ture, Muslim of Manding, and great Berete,
    Muslim of Manding,
And they had to work against Sunjata

Before he left the circumcision area.
The head of the Tures
And the head of the Beretes
Set to work
And prepared *naso*.
When they wrote on the writing-board,
For one month and fourteen days
They wrote on the board – the *bisimalato* pattern.
They prepared names,
They made calculations from God's names
And they put them in the *naso*,
And they added special ingredients,
And then they took it to Susu Sumanguru Baamagana.
They said to him, 'If you put this *naso* in your
    wash-place,
And stop up the mouth of the container for forty days,
When the forty days are up,
If you wash yourself with the *naso*,
And if the child does not see you
And nothing has spoilt the *naso*,
You will die in office,
But this child will never be king here in Manding.
When you have washed yourself with it at midnight,
That night you must come out, wet with that *naso*,
And walk round all four gates of Manding,
And you must walk round all four corners of Manding
That night before dawn breaks.
Then this child,' they said,
'Will never be king.'
During this time,
Sunjata's sister, Nene Faamaga,

Was talking with her spirit king, Yura,
One Friday night.
Manga Yura said to her,
'They have contrived a stratagem against your brother,
And if it succeeds,
Then his prospects of becoming king are destroyed.'
'What sort of a stratagem is it?' she asked.
He told her, 'They are making *naso*,
And they are putting special ingredients in it.
If Susu Sumanguru Baamagana succeeds in washing
     with that *naso*,
If he goes round the four gates of Manding,
If he walks through the town of Manding,
Then Sunjata's prospects of becoming king are
     destroyed.'
She said to him, 'Won't you help us then?
For the sake of love, my life is in your hands,
And you must support us;
We have no mother,
We have no father,
We are orphans,
We have no uncle.'
He replied, 'All right,
On the eve of the appointed day
I shall remove you and Sunjata both from the
     circumcision area
And I shall take you to the wash-place;
When Sumanguru is about to wash himself with the
     naso,
I shall give your father's sword to Sunjata
And he can fall upon Susu Sumanguru Baamagana

And prevent him from washing with the *naso*.
They will fight there in the wash-place.
If that *naso* is spilt,' he said,
'Susu Sumanguru Baamagana's reign will be destroyed,
And nothing will stop Sunjata from becoming king.'
She said, 'Praise be to God.'
He went on, 'Today they have put the *naso* in the
        wash-place;
Thirty-nine days from today,
On the eve of the fortieth day,
I shall come for you and I shall take you to the
        circumcision area,
And I shall take Sunjata out of there,
And I shall take him to the wash-place.
Whatever is needed, I shall give to Sunjata there.'
Sir, it is of Lion that I speak, great stock,
Simbong, it is of Lion that I speak, the man of great stock is
        a man of power.
Praise be to God, Master of the worlds.
. . . .

They sat quietly for thirty-nine days;
On the eve of the fortieth day
Kaata Yura
Arrived at Sunjata's sister's house.
It had just got dark when the spirit king arrived,
Along with his griot and his xylophone.
It was on that occasion that the xylophone made its
        first appearance.
When people had finished their evening meal
And were starting to go to bed,
Sunjata's sister, Nene Faamaga,

And her spirit king,
Manga Yura –
He placed Nene Faamaga upon his back
And flew into the air with her.
They went to the circumcision area
And he covered up the eyes of the man in charge of the
      circumcision area,
And all those in the circumcision area
He put to sleep.
He laid Sunjata upon Nene Faamaga's back
And they flew away to the stronghold.
He deposited Sunjata inside Susu Sumanguru
      Baamagana's wash-place
And he left him standing there.
He went for Sunjata's father's long sword,
And came and put it in Sunjata's hand.
When it was midnight,
They were standing in the wash-place,
And Susu Sumanguru Baamagana and his griot and his
      two attendants came out of the house and into the
      wash-place.
Sumanguru undressed, laid down his amulets,
Sat on a white stone,
Put his hand on top of the jar containing ablution
      water,
And said, 'The head of the Siise family prescribed
Two white chickens as a votive offering.
I gave two white chickens as an offering.
The boy's namesake got the better of my namesake.
The head of the Komma family prescribed
Two white rams as an offering.

I gave two white rams as an offering.
The boy's namesake got the better of my namesake.
The head of the Jaane family prepared
Stone and paper.
I put them in the Niger.
The one bearing my name sank, and the one bearing
    the boy's name came to the surface.
The head of the Tures and the head of the Beretes
Prepared this *naso*,
And they declared that if I wash with it,
Within four days,
If the boy does not see me,
If I walk round the four gates of Manding,
Then when I complete it,
I shall be master of Manding
Till I die,
And Sunjata will never be in control of Manding.'
He put his hand into the *naso*,
And was about to sprinkle it on himself,
When Sunjata swiftly drew his sword
And demanded of him, 'What did you say?'
Sumanguru replied, 'I didn't say anything!'
Sunjata said, 'Yes,
What did you say?'
Sumanguru said, 'I did not speak.'
(In Mandinka that is 'I did not speak'.)
Sunjata demanded, 'What did you say?'
Sumanguru replied, 'I didn't say anything!'
Sunjata ordered, 'Pour it away!', and he poured it
    away.
Sunjata ordered, 'Dig a hole!', and he dug a hole.

Sunjata ordered, 'Put your amulets in it!', and he put
    them in it.
Sunjata ordered, 'Fill it in!', and he filled it in.
Sunjata ordered, 'Urinate on it!', and he urinated on it.
Sunjata said to Sumanguru's griot, 'Sing this man's
    praises, please.'
The griot said, *'Cut and Sirimang,*
It is forging and the left hand,
Senegalese coucal and swallow,
Cut iron with iron,
What makes iron valuable,
Big kuku tree and big silk-cotton tree.'
Sunjata shouted, 'Stop there!'
Then he said, 'Call him by the name Kante – *n kang te.*'
He ordered the griot, 'Now sing my praises, please.'
And the griot said, *'Dugu and Bala,*
Faabaga and Taulajo,
Wuruwarang Kaba,
Dala Kumbukamba,
And Dala Jiibaa Minna,
Kasawura Konte,
Sukulung Kutuma
And Sukulung Yammaru,
Naareng Makhang Konnate,
Cats on the shoulder,
Simbong and Jata are at Naarena,
Bone-breaking Lion,
Tie Manding Simbara
And untie Simbara.'
It was that day that he said:
Thatching grass, thatching grass, thatching grass,

Other things go underneath thatching grass,
Thatching grass does not go underneath anything.
The spirit picked up Sunjata and his sister
And took them to the circumcision area.
They were there till the day when the newly
    circumcised boys were leaving the circumcision
    area;
It was on that day that Sunjata was given his own tune.
His mother,
Sukulung Konte, said
That the child whom she had borne
Had been carried in her womb for twelve years;
Some people had said that it was a disease,
Others had said that it was an illness causing swelling
    of the abdomen,
Others had said that it was worms,
Others had said that it was all sorts of things.
At length she had given birth to that child,
And for fourteen years the child was a cripple;
He just sat, and did not walk.
Was it that child who was coming thus in the attire of a
    newly circumcised boy?
Sunjata has come, Sumanguru,
Sunjata has come, Sumanguru.
Sumanguru was the king who was in control of
    Manding at that time.
Sunjata has come, Sumanguru.
Ah, Sunjata is a cripple,
Sunjata has come, Sumanguru.
Sunjata said:
Thatching grass, thatching grass, thatching grass,

Other things go underneath thatching grass,
Thatching grass does not go underneath anything.
Thatching grass, thatching grass, thatching grass,
Others run away from Sunjata,
Sunjata does not run away from anyone.
A soap-taking dog,
A dog which does not leave soap alone,
It will not leave a bone alone,
Sunjata ding kasi kang, Sumanguru.
Death is better than disgrace, Sumanguru.
Kankinya,
Kankinya, griot, Kankinya,
Kankinya, there is a gate at Kankinya,
War at Kankinya.

Kankinya was Susu Sumanguru's stronghold.
When Sunjata had entered Manding,
That night Susu Sumanguru Baamagana prepared for
     war;
He attacked Sunjata's mother's compound
And burned it to the ground, and he captured Sunjata.
But Sunjata escaped
And went to Mansa Farang Tunkara.
He lived there,
And at night he would sally forth and come into
     Manding;
He would take an army and destroy the whole of one
     area of Manding,
And then retire.
Susu Sumanguru would pursue him,
But when they reached Mansa Farang Tunkara's
     territory,

Sumanguru would turn back.
Sunjata's sister
Was married to a spirit,
Whose name, as you are aware, was Manga Yura.
One day Manga Yura said to his wife,
'If you want to overcome Sumanguru,
You won't do it by fighting.
A spear and an arrow, that is what will kill him.'
Spear and arrow in Mandinka,
If you say spear and arrow,
That is bow and spear.
That spear was in the possession of the head of the
      Sooras.
Jinna Musa came to Sunjata;
He found him at Mansa Farang Tunkara's place.
He gave him a charm,
And told Sunjata that he was to go on pilgrimage to
      Mecca
And he would pray for him till he secured Manding.
Jinna Musa went on pilgrimage to Mecca.
When he returned,
He brought a spear,
The spear Tuluku Muluku, *One place where it enters,*
      nine places where blood comes forth.
They call him Kiliya Musa,
Nooya Musa,
Bula Wuruwuru,
And Bala Wanjaga,
Futu Yokhobila,
Sina Yokhobila,
Bimba Yokhobila,

Baha la nankang *Musa,*
And Fitaga Musa.
He it was who brought the spear, the bow and the
     arrow.
He it was who begat Faa Koli Kumba
And Faa Koli Daaba.
These two people joined Makhang Sunjata,
And they fought alongside him.
They used to come to Manding with him;
They lived at Mansa Farang Tunkara's place.
Sunjata's sister, Nene Faamaga, came and said to him,
'I want you to come to my spirit king
So that he can help you.'
Indeed, it is of Lion that I speak, great stock,
Simbong, it is of Lion that I speak, great stock.
Great God,
Sukulung Kutuma
And Sukulung Yammaru here,
Naareng Makhang Konnate,
Cats on the shoulder,
Simbong and Jata are at Naarena.
In Sunjata's day a griot did not have to fetch water,
To say nothing of farming and gathering firewood.
Father World has changed, changed.
One day when Sunjata had to come to the hill called
     Yura,
The spirit king came with his griot and xylophone.
At that time Bala Faasigi Kuyate
Belonged to Susu Sumanguru Baamagana in Manding.
Sunjata and Faa Koli Kumba and Faa Koli Daaba were
     sitting

87

In his sister's house.
The spirit king, Manga Yura, arrived
With the xylophone, which they played like this –
(This is Manga Yura's tune).
When Sunjata heard the xylophone
He asked his sister,
'What sort of instrument is making that noise?'
She replied, 'It is my husband who is coming with it,
He and his griot, but I don't know what it is.'
Sunjata declared, 'In that case I will kill your husband
     today
And take this instrument.'
She asked, 'Are you going to kill him?'
He answered, 'Yes.'
She said, 'This is the person who helped you.'
Sunjata said, 'I will kill him today.'
They went under the bed.
When the spirit king arrived, he stood in the doorway,
And he said to his wife,
'Nene Faamaga,' and she replied.
He went on, 'I shall not sleep in this house today
Unless I dismantle the bed.'
She said, 'It was my brother who erected this bed,
It is not going to be dismantled.'
He said, 'Ah, Nene Faamaga,
This is the eve of Friday;
I shall not sleep on the bed,
Only on the floor.
I shall pull up the forked sticks supporting the bed,
And lie on the floor.
Nene Faamaga,' he added,

'Nothing happens under the plait which the louse does
    not know about.
Your brother who is lying under the bed –
Tell him to come out.'
Sunjata came out.
The long-barrelled gun which he had
He let fly at the spirit king.
It split apart right to the butt.
The spirit king lay on the bed laughing.
At that time Bala Faasigi Kuyate was a member of Susu
    Sumanguru Baamagana's household.
Faa Koli Kumba came out from under the bed and
    drew an arrow
And fired it at the spirit king;
The arrow shattered completely.
Faa Koli Daaba came out from under the bed with a
    round iron rod,
And he lifted it up and held his two hands up like this.
The spirit king said to Nene Faamaga,
'You have shamed me.
So it is,
The spirits are saying that I have married just an
    insignificant human,
That I have pursued nothing but an insignificant
    human.
If you want the xylophone,
Tell me, and I will give it to your brother,
But I think that my life does not count for as much
    with you as the xylophone does.'
It was that day that Sunjata got the xylophone;
He went away with the xylophone;

He went to Mansa Farang Tunkara's place with it,
And he hung up the xylophone.
No one played it except Sunjata himself.
Susu Sumanguru Baamagana devised a plan
And gave orders that Sunjata be summoned;
When he came to Manding,
They must say to him that he is a prince,
That they are smiths and that they must return the
    land to him;
Since his brothers were in Manding,
He ought not to flee from his father's home
And go and live in the land of the Tunkaras.
They sent Bala Faasigi Kuyate to deliver the summons;
Bala Faasigi Kuyate's name originated from that.
When Bala Faasigi Kuyate arrived,
He explained his mission to Mansa Farang Tunkara
In these words: 'The people of Manding have sent me
With orders to come for Sunjata;
He must go to Manding,
He must go and be king,
Because he is a son of the royal line.
He ought not to run away
And come and live here.'
Sunjata rushed up to him
And declared, 'You have spoken the truth.'
He took down the xylophone,
And Bala Faasigi Kuyate asked him, 'What is this?'
Sunjata answered, 'I myself got this from a relative of
    mine.'
He took down the xylophone and gave it to him.
As soon as Bala Faasigi had played the xylophone,

Sunjata grabbed his two Achilles tendons and cut them,
And he told Bala Faasigi, 'You will not go back again.
You must stay here and play the xylophone for me;
You must be my griot.'
That is why he is called Bala Faasigi;
They cut his tendons and they called him Bala Faasigi –
'You will settle here.'
His name was Musa,
But they called him Bala Faasigi Kuyate;
When they had cut these two tendons,
They told him, 'Settle here!'
That is why they gave him the xylophone.
Sunjata's sister left home
And went to Mansa Farang Tunkara
And told him, 'I have come to my brother
So that he may let me go
And marry Susu Sumanguru Baamagana.
Sumanguru will certainly never know me as a wife,
Since he is a smith.'
After Sunjata's sister
Had said that she was going to marry Susu Sumanguru
    Baamagana,
She came and found Susu Sumanguru and his griots
    sitting.
His griots shouted his praises,
'*Cut and Sirimang,*
It is forging and the left hand,
Senegalese coucal and swallow,
Cut iron with iron,
What makes iron valuable,
Big kuku tree and big silk-cotton tree.'

To Sunjata's sister they said, 'Greetings!',
And she returned the greeting.
Bala Faasigi Kuyate
Said to her,
'Nene Faamaga, what have you come here for?'
She told him, 'I have come to marry Susu Sumanguru
     Baamagana.'
Susu Sumanguru Baamagana raised himself up into a
     sitting position
And asked her, 'What did you say?'
She replied, 'I have come to marry Susu Sumanguru
     Baamagana.'
He asked her, 'What for? –
Your brother and I, Susu Sumanguru Baamagana, are
     enemies;
It is now seven years
That we have been waging war by every available
     means.
Your brother wishes to make himself master of
     Manding;
How comes it that you could marry Susu Sumanguru
     Baamagana?'
She replied, 'I have talked with Sunjata,
But he took no heed of what I said,
Because he is my younger brother,
Whom I have carried upon my back.
Since he refuses to listen to me,
I wash my hands of him,
And I will marry Susu Sumanguru Baamagana,
And my brother will see me in his keeping,
And there is nothing that he will be able to do about it.'

They were married that very day.
When Susu Sumanguru Baamagana and Sunjata's sister
    went to bed at night,
He put his hand on her,
But she removed his hand;
He asked her, 'What is the matter?'
And she answered, 'I am the daughter of a king,
You too are a king;
You will know me as a wife,
But you have not told me about yourself.'
'About myself?' he said.
She said to him, 'You have not told me
What it is that can kill you –
Why then should I marry you?
Why should you know me as a wife?
For what good reason?
Besides, you are a smith, I am a princess.
In fact, I am marrying you because of some magical
    power of yours;
You must tell me what that magical power is,
That power which can kill you.'
He raised his hand and laid it upon her again,
And she said to him, 'Only if you tell me
About yourself!'
He was about to speak
When his mother, who was in the house,
Cleared her throat
And said to him, 'Susu Sumanguru Baamagana,
My child, don't ruin yourself.
Is a one-night woman
Going to destroy your whole world?

You and this woman's brother are at war,
Night and day.
You attack each other with *korte*,
You assail each other through diviners,
And now you say that that man's sister is to marry you,
When she lies down at your back,
You will reveal all about yourself in that one night.'
He said to Nene Faamaga, 'Wait;
When my mother is asleep, I will tell you what you
    want to know.'
She replied, 'All right, when your mother has fallen
    asleep,
And you have told me,
Then will you know me as a wife,
But if you do not tell me how you can be killed,
You will not know me as a wife.'
When his mother had fallen asleep,
He laid his hand upon Nene Faamaga.
She said to him,
'You shall not know me as a wife
Unless you tell me what will kill you.'
He replied, 'A spear will not kill me,
An arrow will not kill me,
A gun will not kill me,
Korte will not kill me,
Witchcraft will not kill me;
There is only one thing,' he said, 'which will kill me:
A one-year-old cock which crows,
Provided it is a white fowl.'
He said, 'You will catch it and kill it,
And you must remove its spur,

And you must put pure gold dust and pure silver dust
    inside it,
And you must put it in a gun.
If you shoot me with that,
I shall die.'
She said to him, 'I shall be menstruating till tomorrow,'
She lay down and they fell asleep.
The cocks crowed;
Nene Faamaga leapt over the town wall and off she
    went.
She found Sunjata at Bala Faasigi Kuyate's house;
She and Bala Faasigi Kuyate arose
And went to Mansa Farang Tunkara's place.
She said, 'Sunjata,
My younger brother,
You can have a little mother,
You can have a little father,
But you cannot have a little elder sister.
I am your older sister, my brother.
As to a means of killing Susu Sumanguru Baamagana,
There is only one thing that will do that:
A one-year-old cock which crows
Must be seized and killed.
Into that cock's spur you must put silver dust and gold
    dust.
You must load a gun with powder and put the spur in
    the gun.
That cock's spur,' she said,
'Is what will kill Susu Sumanguru Baamagana.'
Sunjata said, 'All right.'
He summoned Dala Kumbukamba.

At that time the soldiers who were under Sunjata's
    command:
Jinna Musa's sons,
Faa Koli Kumba
And Faa Koli Daaba,
And Kiliya Musa
And Nooya Musa,
Together with Bala Faasigi Kuyate.
They got ready and they came against Manding.
Sunjata was advised, 'You will not be able to crush
    Manding
Unless you give a live crocodile as a votive offering,
And take it into the town of Manding;
When it has walked about within the town of
    Manding,
You will then be able to crush Manding
And to kill Susu Sumanguru Baamagana.'
Sunjata was perplexed.
So he went to the head of the Bozos
And asked him to help him to obtain a live crocodile.
He caught a live crocodile and brought it.
Sunjata said, 'Who will take this live crocodile into
    Manding for me?'
Faa Koli Kumba and Faa Koli Daaba said to him,
'We will take the live crocodile to Manding.'
At that time people used to make clothing from cloth
    made up of strips sewn together;
When weavers had made a cloth –
That cloth made up of strips sewn together – they used
    to go and sell it.
Faa Koli Kumba bought a cloth,

A very big one,
And he wrapped up the crocodile
And put it at his side;
He wrapped up that cloth,
Tied it and took it to Manding.
When he reached the public meeting place in Manding,
The women saw him and rushed up to him saying,
     'Here is the cloth pedlar!'
He said to them, 'It is already dark;
I shall not sell these cloths till tomorrow.
I am going to sleep here.'
They went and lodged him in a house.
Woliwolinki,
Tambaki great man and Magasugu Ngandana,
Great Bula is cold.
That refers to the head of the Sooras,
Kiliya Musa and Nooya Musa,
Bula Wuruwuru and Bula Wanjaga,
Kutu Yokhobila and Sina Yokhobila,
And Bumbang Yokhobila.
That is Faa Koli Kumba
And Faa Koli Daaba
They fought in Manding with spear and arrow for
     Sunjata.
They went and lodged him.
After he had gone to bed, when night had fallen and
     midnight come,
He saddled his horse;
He took the cloth and tied it on his horse,
He shut the door and left the live crocodile inside the
     house.

The diviners by stones and the diviners by cowries had
    told
Susu Sumanguru Baamagana,
'No one can kill you here
Unless he gives a live crocodile as an offering,
And it walks about inside the town of Manding.
The man who would catch a live crocodile and bring it
    into Manding
Has never been seen by us,
Because we would kill anyone who entered here.'
Sunjata left there and went to Mansa Farang Tunkara's
    place,
Where he met a man who owned 'black medicine',
Who said to him, 'Koro ming kankang, dung koro ning
    baajii, foroko fila ning falang.'
He said, 'I will prepare a black cat's skin
And make *korte* out of it;
That black cat's skin
Must you take and go to Manding
And give to someone who will drop it down the well
    in Manding.'
Dawn broke; the women jostled each other
As they brought a huge breakfast
For Faa Koli Kumba and Faa Koli Daaba in his house.
When they opened the door the live crocodile
Came waddling out of the house.
There was a commotion, and the drums were sounded;
Men said, 'Susu Sumanguru Baamagana,
The stranger who slept here last night
Brought a crocodile into this town as a votive offering.'
They caught the crocodile

And tied it up;
Faa Koli Kumba and Faa Koli Daaba
Came with his spear that day to Manding;
He said to Sunjata, 'The black cat's skin –
They killed a black cat and made it into a leather bag
    and put *naso* in it.
If someone takes that *naso*
And drops it down the well of Manding,
That Manding well which is in the middle of the town,
The day that he drops it down there,
And that the people of Manding drink water from that
    well,
That day will you crush Manding.'
When the drums sounded, all the people of Manding
    gathered at the public meeting-place,
By one of their gatehouses;
They were sitting near that well;
They had tied up the live crocodile and laid it down.
Susu Sumanguru Baamagana arose and declared,
'Whoever finds the trader
Who brought this crocodile here into this town
Must seize him and bring him here.'
He would divide Manding into two parts,
And he would give one part to the man who found the
    trader, and he would be in control of it.
Sibi Kamara, head of the Kamaras, arose –
That head of the Kamaras, Sibi Kamara,
Begat Hamana Kamara,
And he begat also Baliya Kamara.
Baliya Kamara begat Foobali Dumbe,
Foobali Dumbe begat Makhang Kuta Kamara,

Makhang Kuta Kamara begat Juhuna Kamara,
Juhuna Kamara begat Tamba Bukari,
Tamba Bukari begat Soona Kamara,
Soona Kamara bore Almami Samori.

Sibi Kamara declared that he would go and fetch the
    person
Who had brought the crocodile there.
He would seek him out,
With fetish he would seek him out,
With *korte* he would seek him out,
With the help of a diviner by stones he would seek him
    out.
They were just at that point
When Soora Musa Bankang [Faa Koli],
Kiliya Musa and Nooya Musa,
Bula Wuruwuru and Bula Wanjaga,
Arrived on horseback with the bag made out of a black
    cat.
He came and found the people sitting at the public
    meeting-place.
He galloped past
And came upon some women beside the well;
He spurred his white stallion,
Which raised its two forelegs
And placed them on the low wall surrounding the well;
He put his hand into his leather bag
And withdrew the black cat's skin,
And declared: 'People of Manding,
I am Soora Musa Bankang,
Kiliya Musa and Nooya Musa, Bula Wuruwuru.
It was Sunjata who sent me,

With orders to throw this black cat's skin as an offering
Down your well.'
He threw it down the well.
There was an uproar and the drum sounded.
They rushed upon him and he spurred his white
    stallion.
He had a spear that day
And the name of that spear was Tuluku Muluku, *One*
    place where it enters, nine places where the blood comes
    out.
When you hear people called Soora, their surname is
    Susokho.
He spurred his horse.
When he spurred his horse with the stirrups,
The horse leapt up with him;
Whenever he struck anyone a single blow with the
    spear,
If he pierced him in one place,
Blood would come out of nine places altogether in his
    body.
Finally he went right through the crowd
And out at the other side;
He went and found Sunjata at Bala Faasigi Kuyate's
    place.
He found Bala Faasigi Kuyate and Sunjata sitting;
He said to them, 'I have washed the black cat.
I have thrown it down the well.
I found the people sitting with a live crocodile at the
    four gates of Manding.'
Bala Faasigi Kuyate arose and shouted,
'*Sukulung Kutuma*

And Sukulung Yammaru,
Naareng Makhang Konnate,
Cats on the shoulder,
Simbong and Jata are at Naarena,
Bone-breaking Lion,
Tie Manding Simbara and untie Manding Simbara,
Dugu and Bala,
Faabaga and Taulajo,
Mighty horseman whom none surpasses,
Wuruwarang Kaba,
Dala Kumbukamba,
And Dala Jiibaa Minna,
Sankarang Madiba Konte,
He it was who was the father of Sukulung Konte
She it was who bore you, Makhang Sunjata.'
Sunjata arose,
And went and seized a white cock that day,
And killed it.
When he had killed the white cock,
They plucked it and singed it;
They burned its feet and removed the spurs,
They put silver dust and gold dust inside,
They loaded a gun and put it in the hands of Faa Koli
    Kumba and Faa Koli Daaba.
They came and circled round Manding, the three of
    them,
Faa Koli Kumba and Faa Koli Daaba and Sunjata;
Seven times they went round Manding, then they
    stood still,
They and Bala Faasigi Kuyate.
It was that day that Bala Faasigi Kuyate sang:

Ah, Sunjata has come, Sumanguru,
Ah, Sunjata has come, Sumanguru.
The town drum sounded.
Ah, Sunjata has come, Sumanguru,
Ah, Sunjata is here, Sumanguru.
They sounded the town drum and the whole town
      came forth.
Sunjata, with his horse,
And his long sword,
And his iron rod,
And his double-barrelled gun with the cock's spur in it.
Susu Sumanguru Baamagana came forth,
With his long sword,
And his iron rod,
And his three-pronged spear,
And his double-barrelled gun.
All of Manding came forth;
They stood at the four wondrous gates,
And they sent forth these two men.
Sunjata said to Susu Sumanguru Baamagana, 'Go
      ahead.'
Susu Sumanguru Baamagana replied, 'No, you go
      ahead, you are the younger.'
Sunjata answered, 'No, go ahead, you are the older.'
Susu Sumanguru Baamagana took his horse back some
      distance, then he declared: 'This is far enough.'
He charged on horseback with his three-pronged spear;
He raised it aloft and struck Sunjata with it;
The three-pronged spear shattered and fell to the
      ground.
Sumanguru retired;

There was a great shout.
Faa Koli Kumba and Faa Koli Daaba and Bala Faasigi
    Kuyate,
Only these three were in support of Sunjata,
Whereas the whole of Manding supported Susu
    Sumanguru Baamagana.
After Susu Sumanguru Baamagana had struck Sunjata
He retired and went a long way off on his horse,
Then he returned.
He struck Sunjata with his long sword;
The long sword broke into three pieces and fell to the
    ground.
He retired again
Then returned with his iron rod.
He raised it aloft and was about to strike Sunjata with
    the iron rod,
But his arm remained aloft, immovable.
He said to Sunjata, 'Go ahead.'
Sunjata came and struck Sumanguru with his
    three-pronged spear;
The three-pronged spear was shattered.
He retired, then came with a long sword;
The long sword too was shattered and fell to the
    ground.
When he set his hand to his gun
And raised it and was about to aim at him,
It was then that Susu Sumanguru Baamagana turned tail
And was about to run away.
Sunjata declared:
Sunjata has come, Sumanguru,
Ah, Sunjata is here, Sumanguru.

He went on:
Thatching grass, thatching grass, thatching grass,
Other things go underneath thatching grass,
Thatching grass does not go underneath anything;
Thatching grass, thatching grass, thatching grass,
Others run away from Sunjata,
Sunjata does not run from anyone.
A soap-taking dog,
A dog which does not leave soap alone
Will not leave a bone alone.
Sunjata ding kasi kang, Sumanguru,
Death is better than disgrace, Sumanguru.

He produced the chicken spur at that point
And shot Sumanguru with it;
He fell.
It was that day that Sunjata told Bala Faasigi Kuyate,
'Every smith in Manding
Will bear the name Nkante.
I want you to sing the praises of the smiths so that
    I can hear.'
He declared:
Cut and Sirimang.
It is forging and the left hand,
Senegalese coucal and swallow,
Cut iron with iron,
What makes iron valuable,
Big kuku tree and big silk-cotton tree,
Fari and Kaunju.
As the Mandinka say, the eastern people understand
    the language of the griots;
All this is meaningful.

He said, 'Sege and Sirimang,
That is Sunjata and Susu Sumanguru Baamagana.
That is forging and the left hand –
That is pincers and iron.
Cut iron with iron, what makes iron valuable –
That means that one great man gets the better of
      another great man by magical means.
Big kuku *tree and big silk-cotton tree –*
That means that however big a silk-cotton tree may be,
      it stands in an even bigger open space.
Fari and Kaunju –
That is the bellows and the small clay mound through
      which the bellows pipe leads into the fire.'

He turned round and presented his back;
Sunjata was standing.
Bala said, '*Dugu and Bala,*
Faabaga and Taulajo,
Supreme horseman whom none surpasses,
Wuruwarang Kaba,
Dala Kumbukamba and Dala Jiibaa Minna,
Kasawura Konte,
Sankarang Madiba Konte,
He it was who was the father of Sukulung Konte,
Sukulung Konte it was who bore you, Makhang Sunjata.'
He went on,
It is war which devastated Manding,
It is war which rebuilt Manding.
Sunjata entered Manding with these griots' songs.
They sang:
Kankinya,

Kankinya, there is a gate at Kankinya,
Kankinya, there is a gate at Kankinya,
War at Kankinya.
The fortified position occupied by Susu Sumanguru
    Baamagana
Was called Kankinya.
When Sunjata entered Manding,
He destroyed the four wondrous gates;
He rebuilt them and made them into four gatehouses,
He made them into four gatehouses;
Four little beds were put inside them.
When dawn broke,
Bala Faasigi Kuyate would come
And play this tune – the *Janjungo* tune.
At first cock-crow
He would come and stand at Sunjata's gate;
He would play the *Janjungo* tune and say:
Great Janjung, it is war which shattered Janjung,
War rebuilt great Janjung.
Janjung was the name of that Manding gatehouse.
He would say to Sunjata,
'*Sukulung Kutuma*
And Sukulung Yammaru here,
Nareng Makhang Konnate,
Cats on the shoulder,
Simbong and Jata are at Naarena.
In Sunjata's day a griot did not have to fetch water,
To say nothing of farming and gathering firewood.
Father World has changed, changed.'
Sunjata would come out of his house
And come and sit on his earthen platform

Near his own doorway.
Bala would go and stand by the head of the Sooras
And he would say to him, '*Soora Musa Bankaalu,*
Kiliya Musa and Nooya Musa,
Bula Wuruwuru and Bula Wanjaga,
Kutu Yokhobila and Sina Yokhobila,
And Karta Yokhobila and Bumba Yokhobila.
It was your grandfather who sounded the royal drum to
     summon assemblies,
Mighty Bagadugu and Ginate,
Mighty Hanjugu and Hamina Yanga.'
The head of the Sooras would also come out
And come and sit on his earthen platform.
(At that time wooden platforms for sitting on were not
     built;)
They used to beat earth into a platform,
Which they called *bilingo*.
Each of the four gates had an earthen platform.
He would go to Faa Koli Kumba and to Faa Koli
     Daaba,
He would go to Sibi Kamara,
And the latter would also come and sit at his
     gatehouse.
Bala Faasigi Kuyate would come and sit in their midst.
Sunjata was in control of Manding for seven years.
. . . .

Now, white man, the account of Sunjata's career as far
     as I know it,
As I heard it from my parents,
And my teachers,
Ends here.